**The thoughts she wa:
far from steady. And
professional.**

Dani's mind raced, despite her attempts to bring herself back to reason. She breathed in the last traces of cinnamon in the air and imagined that Cade *hadn't* let go. What would it feel like, for the top of her head to rest in the hollow beneath his chin? For his stubble to graze her forehead? Her skin felt hot as she thought of quite a few other sensations she'd like to have while Cade held her... kissed her...and perhaps did more than kiss her.

Stop. This was pointless. She and Cade worked together, and she couldn't be effective at work if she was distracted by her attraction to a colleague.

Attraction. That was all it was. It couldn't be anything more. For one thing, she had no idea if Cade felt anything for her. And even if he did, it would probably evaporate the moment he learned the full truth about her.

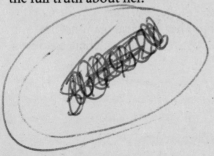

Dear Reader,

Medical romance lets me write about a dilemma close to my heart—how can you relax and let loose when everyone's depending on you?

As twelfth in line to the throne of Lorovia, Dr. Dani DuMaria is all too familiar with the weight of responsibility. Her family has allowed her to pursue her dream of practicing medicine, but now that she's completed her residency, she's expected to resume her role in the royal family.

But when Dani impresses Dr. Cade Logan during a medical emergency, he offers her the chance of a lifetime—a fellowship at a hospital in the Caribbean! Cade's well-muscled arms and ocean-blue eyes are hard to resist, and Dani convinces her family to let her continue her medical career…on the condition that she keep her royal status a secret.

But some secrets are difficult to keep. Like the secret of Dani's attraction to Cade, who's sworn off relationships because of his own complicated past. When the two of them attempt a clandestine, no-strings-attached fling, Dani must decide whether she'll continue to put her royal obligations first…or whether she'll follow her dream of a chance at love.

Hope you enjoy!

Warmly,

Julie Danvers

JulieDanvers.WordPress.com

THE PRINCESS WHO STOLE HIS HEART

JULIE DANVERS

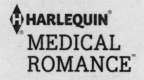

HARLEQUIN®
MEDICAL
ROMANCE™

Recycling programs
for this product may
not exist in your area.

ISBN-13: 978-1-335-73790-8

The Princess Who Stole His Heart

Harlequin Enterprises ULC
22 Adelaide St. West, 41st Floor
Toronto, Ontario M5H 4E3, Canada
www.Harlequin.com

Printed in U.S.A.

Julie Danvers grew up in a rural community surrounded by farmland. Although her town was small, it offered plenty of scope for imagination, as well as an excellent library. Books allowed Julie to have many adventures from her own home, and her love affair with reading has never ended. She loves to write about heroes and heroines who are adventurous, passionate about a cause, and looking for the best in themselves and others. Julie's website is juliedanvers.wordpress.com.

Books by Julie Danvers

Harlequin Medical Romance

Portland Midwives
The Midwife from His Past

From Hawaii to Forever
Falling Again in El Salvador
Secret from Their LA Night

Visit the Author Profile page at Harlequin.com.

To WAB, the best online writing group
a girl could ask for.

CHAPTER ONE

A MILLION DISTRACTIONS vied for Dani's attention in the busy ER. She fought to tune out the chatter of nurses, snippets of conversation from patients and the pounding from the construction work that had gone on all summer and never seemed to end.

Dani let the noise fade into the background as she reviewed the chart in front of her, hastily jotting notes into a pad. It was the last day of her residency in internal medicine, and she was determined to arrive prepared for rounds. She was scheduled to present on a patient, and Dr. Benson, the senior training physician, had a reputation for challenging residents with difficult questions. Dani had seen trainees leave rounds in tears because of his gruff, intimidating manner.

But Dr. Benson hadn't made Dani cry yet, and she was determined that he never would. She had every intention of finishing her residency with her reputation for withstanding Dr. Benson's intense gaze—known as the Benson Glare—intact.

Despite Dani's focus, one sound rose above the general hubbub and penetrated her concentration. A sharp cough, followed by a gasp, as though someone couldn't get enough air. It was the gasp that made her look up sharply and scan the ER.

Boston General Hospital was an extremely old building, which meant construction was constantly taking place somewhere. As Dani looked for the source of the gasping cough, she saw that a construction worker had dropped his hammer and was hunched over, catching his breath. When he noticed Dani watching him, he gave a quick, reassuring nod and wiped his forehead, then retrieved his hammer and returned to work.

Dani hesitated to return to her notes. Something about the man's cough hadn't sounded right to her. But he seemed to be returning to work without any trouble. And none of the other doctors and nurses in the ER seemed to notice anything amiss. She looked back at the chart in front of her.

Only to have it slammed shut by her best friend, Kim, who bounced up to the nurses' station with her usual exuberance.

"Hey!" Dani protested. "I was reading that!"

"Of course you were." Kim's dark eyes sparkled with mischief. "Only you would be studiously brushing up on patients on the last day of residency. Don't you think there are more important things to do?"

Dani pulled at the locks of her chestnut ponytail, as she always did when she felt fretful. "What's more important than preparing for rounds?"

"Hmm…" Kim pretended to think. "How about taking some time to say good-bye to dear old Boston General? Saying thanks to the senior doctors who've mentored us, the nurses who've kept us from screwing up…and, most importantly, planning all the drinks and get-togethers that need to happen before our residency cohort scatters across the country to begin the next phase of their careers?"

For a moment, Dani almost felt tears prick at her eyelids, but she tried to hide them with a forced smile. Kim was too perceptive not to notice.

"Oof, sorry, Dani. I didn't mean to bring that up. I just meant to say…don't work so hard that you forget to say good-bye to everyone."

"It's okay. You don't need to be afraid to mention it—it's no secret that I'm not taking a position anywhere. I've accepted it. I'm just sad that everyone's leaving Boston in a few weeks."

"I still can't believe you don't have a job or a fellowship lined up. You're one of the best residents in our program."

Dani tried to appreciate her friend's compliment, but her feelings were bittersweet. After three years of residency in internal medicine, the rest of her cohort was about to leave Boston. Most would begin fellowships in their chosen specialty areas, while others had found positions in hospitals and private practices around the country. Kim would be in Miami for an oncology fellowship. All of Dani's friends were about to take the next major step forward in their medical careers.

But not Dani Martin. Or rather, not Princess Danielle-Genevieve Matthieu DuMaria, twelfth in line to the throne of Lorovia. Dani's home was a tiny country on the north coast of the Mediterranean Sea, nestled between France, Monaco and Italy. What Lorovia lacked in size, it made up for in wealth, as the third-richest country in the world. The chances of Dani ever ruling were miniscule—she was the youngest daughter of a youngest son—but her royal duties were still significant enough to interfere with her medical career.

Dani had told her friends and supervisors that

family obligations prevented her from continuing to practice as a physician, but no one knew just how extensive those obligations were. When she'd announced her intention to enter medical school, a pitched battle had ensued amongst her family members. No one in the royal family had ever had a profession before, and most of her family members were convinced that Dani's royal duties would keep her far too busy to allow her time for a career in medicine. Studying medicine would be tantamount to turning her back on her family and her country.

Dani loved her family, and it hurt when her uncle accused her of abandoning her responsibilities. But becoming a doctor had been Dani's dream since she was fourteen, when a bad fall from a horse had resulted in numerous injuries, including a compound fracture in her leg that required two surgeries. She'd been inspired by the physicians who cared for her and she formed the dream of one day helping others in the same way her own doctors had helped her. During her university years, she decided she wanted to be a cardiologist—after all, the heart powered everything.

Dani's parents supported her dream, even though many of her older family members had reservations. After a week of arguing, the family agreed on a compromise: Dani would be allowed to attend medical school in the United States, where there was less emphasis on European politics and therefore less of a chance that Dani would be recognized as a member of the Lorovian royal family. Her family insisted she keep her status as a princess a strict secret, for security purposes, and that she use the family pseudonym of 'Martin' as her surname. In return, they allowed her to complete her three-year residency in internal medicine immediately after medical school, so that she could have the chance to practice as a full-fledged physician and give back to the medical community. But when Dani finished her residency, she was expected to return home. She would set medicine aside and focus on responsibilities more relevant to her royal status.

Dani hated that her medical career had an expiration date. Quitting after residency meant that she would never be able to pursue a specialty like cardiology, because of the years of extra training that were required. But that was part of the sacrifice of royal birth. If she couldn't have her whole dream, she would have to settle for having part of it.

Her family's status impacted everything from her friendships to her love life. She'd only made a few forays into romance, but she'd had enough experiences to learn that trying to date as a royal was fraught with problems. If she dated someone who knew she was a princess, she could never be certain they liked her for herself and not for her family's power and influence.

Several years ago, at university, she'd come close to giving her heart to someone entirely. Peter. He hadn't known at first that she was a princess. But she'd had to tell him eventually, and when he found out, everything had changed. His family, once extremely wealthy, was facing troubles on public and financial fronts. Peter seemed to view her royal status as the solution to his family's problems. Dani would have supported Peter wholeheartedly, but no matter what she offered, it was never enough. When he went so far as to sell pictures he'd taken of her to a salacious tabloid—pictures he'd promised no one would see but him—Dani knew it was over.

Her heart still stung at his betrayal, even though so much time had passed. After that, she'd made the decision not to reveal her status as a princess unless someone had earned her absolute trust. Only a few of the medical staff at Boston General and Kim knew the truth.

Keeping her princess status a secret for the past several years had been a welcome change. She'd made friends who she knew were true friends, not people who attached themselves to her simply because she was a royal. It was still easier to avoid dating entirely, even though she still couldn't let go of the hope that she might someday meet someone who made her feel special and maybe even fall in love. It was a nice dream, even though it was incredibly unlikely. Even aside from the complications of dating as a royal, Peter's betrayal had hurt her deeply, and she couldn't imagine ever trusting someone with her heart again.

Now, with the time to honor her promise to her family fast approaching, she'd have to stop indulging in dreams. No matter whether she dreamed of falling in love or having a career she loved, the result was the same: as a princess, her life was not her own. In a few weeks, she'd be back to the life of a princess, and her medical career would dissolve into a distant memory.

Dani hated good-byes and preparing for rounds was a welcome distraction. She wanted to make this last presentation her best. After all, it would probably be the last time she ever had a chance to discuss a patient with a group of colleagues.

The sharp cough she'd heard a moment ago echoed across the waiting room again, followed by a longer gasp this time. Dani and Kim both looked up. The construction worker in the corner was half standing, hunched over his bent legs.

"Think he's okay?" asked Dani.

Kim looked uncertain. "None of the nurses seem to be alarmed. And he's still breathing."

The man took another labored draw for breath.

"That's not breathing. That's gasping," Dani said as the man toppled to the ground.

Dani dashed across the waiting room. The man was pale and rapidly losing consciousness. She couldn't feel a pulse.

"He's in cardiac arrest," she told Kim. "Get help."

Kim ran off to call the code.

Instinct took over and Dani acted. She placed her hands on the man's chest, her elbows locked, and began compressions. The alarm she'd felt seconds ago began to melt away as a combination of training and adrenaline took over her body. She ran through proper procedure in her head as she worked, which always helped her to feel more grounded in a crisis. *Push at a depth of two inches. Interlock your fingers. Make sure they don't touch the ribs. Start with thirty chest compressions.*

Relief flooded through her as an emergency team arrived. They'd probably only taken seconds to get there, though it had seemed much longer.

The team consisted of several nurses and a doctor she didn't recognize. He was younger than most of the other doctors, with sun-streaked hair and a stubbled beard. Dani wondered if he might be a new staff member. If so, this was hardly the time for introductions. He merely nodded at her and said, "You're doing great. Keep going until we get to the cath lab."

The team lifted the patient onto the gurney. Dani straddled the man and continued compressions while a nurse delivered oxygen through a bag ventilator. The gurney sped through the ER doors and down the hall to the cardiac catheterization lab as Dani fought to keep her balance and give compressions at the same time.

Dani's arms were shaking by the time they reached the cath lab, though the journey couldn't have taken long. She was so focused on counting compressions that she barely heard the sandy-haired doctor. He had to shake her arm, gently, to get her attention.

"You can stop now," he said. "We're getting him hooked up to an AED."

He held out one hand to help her from the gurney, and for a quick moment Dani was in his arms as he lifted her bodily down to the floor. Doctor Whoever-He-Was had some serious muscles underneath those scrubs.

But she barely had time to consider those muscles or to be shocked at herself for having such a thought at *such* a moment. Because by the time her feet hit the floor, he was already saying, "We've got it from here. Can someone take her outside?"

Dani felt herself guided from the room by a nurse. She stood outside the cath lab, the patient lost to view as the emergency team crowded around him.

After three years of residency, Dani had learned to expect the unexpected. But it was still a shock to see how quickly the situation had gone from normal to critical. One minute the construction worker had been hammering away at the floor. The next, he'd been in cardiac arrest. His life had changed in an instant. Assuming, of course, that he was going to live. She'd only have been in the way if she'd stayed in the cath lab, but she wished she'd gotten the handsome mystery doctor's name. It would have given her some way to follow up with the patient.

As if on cue, the cath lab doors swung open and the unknown doctor stepped out. "Good, you're still here," he said. Now that she could see him outside of a scene of complete chaos, Dani grew more certain that he wasn't from anywhere in Boston. His hair wasn't just light, but bleached in places, as though he spent a lot of time in the sun. His arms were tanned as well—and all signs indicated that she'd been right about those muscles.

"That was pretty heroic for your last day of residency, doc."

How did he know she was a resident? Dani had assumed he was a new staff member, unfamiliar with the hospital. "I don't think we've met," she said.

He smiled, and when he did, one eye closed ever so slightly, as though he were winking at her. "I'm Dr. Logan. Cade Logan." He stuck a hand out for her to shake.

Something was making it a little hard for Dani to get her words out, and if she hadn't had adrenaline coursing through her veins a moment ago, she might have suspected that it had a lot to do with Cade Logan's wink and the warmth of his hand as he shook hers. As it was, she felt as though she could barely force the words out of her throat as she replied, "Dani Martin."

"Well, Dr. Martin, I'm pleased to let you know that thanks to your quick thinking, your patient is on the road to recovery. He's very lucky you happened to be nearby when he went into cardiac arrest—and that you recognized what was happening."

"He's going to be all right?"

"We've done a catheterization to stabilize him for now. He's first on the schedule for a triple bypass tomorrow. It could have been much, much worse if his heart problems had continued to go undetected. It probably saved his life that he happened to go into arrest while working on a construction project in an ER. Seconds counted in a case like this. The fact that you took action immediately gave us valuable extra time."

Dani breathed out, relieved.

"You've managed to do two things today that don't happen often—help to save a life and impress me."

"I'm just glad I was in the right place at the right time," she said.

"Come on, give yourself credit where it's due. CPR, performed competently, at just the right time can make the difference between giving a patient a lifesaving operation, or sending him straight to the morgue. You jumped in when needed, and you had the skills to back up your confidence."

She nodded, letting herself appreciate his words as the familiar bittersweet feeling washed over her. She should appreciate that she'd done well today, even though it would be her last chance to jump into action during a medical emergency.

As though he had a knack for guessing the subject she least wanted to talk about, Cade pressed onward. "Boston General seems about to lose one of their best. May I ask which fellowship you're headed off to, now that your residency is over?"

She hesitated. Even with years to get used to the idea that her career had an expiration date, it was still difficult to talk about. "I'm not going on to a fellowship."

The surprise in his eyes was the same surprise she'd seen in the eyes of her supervisors when they learned she had no plans to specialize as a physician.

"Will you be working as a generalist, then?"

"No. I won't be working at all. Today isn't just my last day of residency. It's my last day as a physician, full stop. I have family obligations that will make it far too difficult to continue."

The concern in his eyes seemed genuine. "I'm so sorry. Is everyone in your family all right?"

"It's nothing like that. My family is… Being in my family means being committed to the family…business. It takes up a lot of time."

"It must be a large business. Are you some kind of pharmaceutical heiress?" His voice was half-teasing, but she saw genuine curiosity in his eyes.

"Something like that." She hated to outright lie to anyone, but misleading Cade Logan wouldn't hurt anyone; she'd probably never see him again after today.

"That's a shame," he said. "The world needs good doctors. Frankly, more than it needs pharmaceutical heiresses."

He was joking, but she could also hear the truth in his voice, behind his smile. Perhaps she could hear it because part of her agreed with him. If she could make her own choices, she'd decide to stick with medicine in a heartbeat.

But her family needed her, and her choices weren't her own.

And who was he to judge her situation before he even knew anything about it?

"Unfortunately, my decision's already been made," she said curtly, hoping that he'd take the hint that she no longer wished to discuss the matter.

"I understand, but…"

"There's no *but*. I need to be there for my family. End of story." She hadn't meant for her words to come out with so much heat, but she was surprised that Cade was pushing her for answers. Usually, people backed off when she explained that family responsibilities kept her from maintaining a medical career. Only Kim had pried further, and that was after she'd become a trusted friend.

He held up a hand. "Okay. Family first. I get

it. But answer me this—why put so much work into becoming a doctor, only to have to walk away after such a short time… What was the point if you were only going to quit?"

She didn't owe Cade any explanations—she'd only just met him, after all. But she found she wanted to answer his question as much for herself as for him. In the toughest times during medical school and residency, she'd found herself wondering why she was putting herself through the sleepless nights, the endless stress of worrying over patients, if she didn't plan to commit to medicine for the rest of her life. But the answer she came back to was always the same.

"Because medicine is a miracle," she said. "It's full of miracles—birth, recovery from illness, overcoming impossible odds. It's science, of course…but there's no other field where you get to see something miraculous every day. Even if I only get to see those miracles for a short time in my life, it's better than never getting to experience them at all. No matter what happens in the future, I'll always look at life differently because I was a doctor. Even if I'm not practicing, I'll know what a miracle it is for a human body to exist, especially one that's suffered through illness or injury. Medicine has showed me that people go on living even under the most extraordinary circumstances, and I'll never forget that."

He was looking at her with an odd expression, as though she'd said something completely unexpected. Suddenly she felt foolish for rambling on about miracles. He probably thought she was hopelessly naive. Nevertheless, it was what she believed.

"And is that enough for you?" he asked. "To have just a few years' worth of memories of all these miracles you've witnessed?"

No. Of course not. She loved medicine. Practicing for just a few years would never be enough. But a princess had a duty to make the best out of the situation she was in. She tilted her chin up and looked straight into his eyes. Blue with flecks of green, giving the effect of an aqua hue. His expression was thoughtful, penetrating. Challenging. She'd met with enough of those expressions during her training that this one didn't faze her.

"It'll have to be," she replied.

She waited for him to tell her that she was utterly ridiculous but, instead, he said, "You're very passionate about medicine for someone who's about to leave it."

"I care about a lot of things. Unfortunately, sometimes those things get in the way of one another."

"For example, your family and your career."
She nodded, glad that he understood.

"Do you know why I'm here in Boston?"

"I assumed you were a visiting physician."

"Not exactly. I'm a fellow in my last year of a unique cardiology fellowship program at the Coral Bay Medical Center on St. Camille—it's an island in the Caribbean."

"I've heard of St. Camille." The island had a reputation for aquamarine waters and white sand beaches. And cardiology was the specialty she'd dreamed of pursuing in her wildest moments—but cardiology had never been an option, with its requirement of an additional three years of training beyond residency.

"There's a need for experienced doctors in St. Camille, but recruiting the right people is a challenge. Lots of students attend medical school in the Caribbean and then want to move back to their home countries once they finish their studies. Not many want to do it the other way around. It's difficult to convince top-talent trainees that it's worth it to move to a small island with limited opportunities."

She nodded. "So you're here on a recruiting mission."

"Exactly. I'm looking for qualified residents, but qualifications aren't enough. The program needs residents who have passion for their work. Residents like you, for example."

"Me?" she was stunned. For one wild moment, she tried to imagine her uncles' reactions if she told them she was planning to spend the next several years in the Caribbean. They'd complained often enough that Boston was too far from Lorovia. St. Camille would be out of the question. "I couldn't. I'm sorry, but…it just isn't possible. My family needs me."

"Of course," he said. "I knew it was a long shot. But if you change your mind, give me a call. There would be an interview, of course, and you'd need strong recommendations from your supervisors. But I have a feeling you'd be a shoo-in."

He smiled again and she felt a pang inside. The way those blue eyes of his almost seemed to sparkle when he smiled… It reminded her of the last time she'd seen the light from the sun hit ocean waves.

His eyes reminded her of home, of all places. She wasn't able to visit as often as she wanted to, but she made sure to return at least once a year during the holidays. It had been several months since she'd walked along the Lorovian coastline, but she could see the water shimmer in her memory as clearly as though she'd been there yesterday.

How odd, she thought, that she could be here in Boston, listening to Cade speak of the Caribbean, and be reminded of home.

Those eyes of his didn't seem to miss much. They might sparkle, but they were penetrating, too. Dani had a small, nearly imperceptible scar just above her upper lip—a remnant from a riding accident when she was young. Most people didn't notice it. But she could feel his eyes on her, tracing the shape of her lips, noticing that something wasn't right.

Why was he looking at her lips that way? It was just a scar. It was imperceptible in photos. Most people didn't notice it unless she pointed it out first—which she rarely did, because she was a little self-conscious about it.

In fact, maybe her self-consciousness was the reason she assumed he was looking at her lips at all. Perhaps he was simply trying to find some feature of hers that stood out, the same way she sometimes tried to make note of a mustache or a pair of glasses when she met someone new and thought she might not remember their name later.

Still, she wasn't used to having her lips stared at with such intensity. She groped for something to say that could end the pause in their conversation, which felt as though it was growing by the second. "What's it like? Living on a tiny island in the Caribbean?"

He raised his eyebrows. "Don't tell me I actually have a shot of reeling you in."

"No, no. I'm just curious."

"In my extremely biased opinion—the word 'paradise' doesn't do it justice."

"But you must live far from your family, unless they're from the island. Isn't that difficult?"

She was surprised by the shadow that passed over his face at the word "family."

"The program is very flexible. There are lots of options to travel home for those who want to. And for some of us, the island's remote location is one of its biggest perks."

Biggest perks? How could that be possible? Dani couldn't imagine living on an island without regularly scheduled trips to see her brothers and cousins. "And what about for you?" she couldn't help asking. "Do you consider the distance a 'perk'?"

"This is the first time I've left the island in six years. Let's just say the distance from family is an asset rather than a liability."

"You haven't left in *six years*?" Dani tried to imagine it. She'd spent so much of her life ruled by family obligations, family history, family traditions. Every decision she'd ever made was influenced by how it would affect her family. And even though she often felt confined by tradition, her family meant everything to her. She couldn't imagine what life would be like without them.

Was family not a priority for Cade? "There must be someone you miss. Family members or...someone important."

"I have everything I need on St. Camille. But the program is very supportive of those who want to visit home." His voice was firm, and Dani had the distinct feeling the subject was closed. Her curiosity burned. Cade had seemed so warm, so relaxed just a moment ago. Right up until the subject of family had arisen.

Of course, family could be a touchy subject for many. Dani of all people could understand that. But to think of Cade going for six years without seeing his family? It was...it was...

It was none of her business. "I didn't mean to pry," she said.

"It's normal to be curious. But...from what you've said about your family obligations, I'm guessing your curiosity isn't strong enough to get you to seriously consider applying."

She gave him a rueful smile. "It sounds like a great program." That was an understatement. It sounded like the perfect program. The kind of adventure she'd jump right into if her life were her own.

But a princess didn't go back on her word. Even if she was presented with one last chance to become the doctor she'd always wanted to be. Even if that chance was presented by someone with light, wavy hair, bleached blond by the sun.

"It's just…with my family situation, it's out of the question."

He shrugged. "Well, I had to try." He shook her hand. "Maybe our paths will cross again sometime."

"I hope so," she said, although she knew he was just saying it to be nice. What were the chances of ever seeing him again when he lived on St. Camille? Especially when he seemed to have little to no interest in leaving the island.

He turned and headed back into the OR, leaving her standing in the hallway.

A princess always did her duty. She'd done the right thing by turning him down. She'd fulfilled her obligations and kept her promise.

So why did she feel as though she'd made a terrible mistake?

One week later, Dani stood outside a bar across the street from Boston General. She and her friends had shared many drinks there over the years, and they'd planned one last gathering before everyone left Boston.

She could already see a few of her friends

inside, but she couldn't bring herself to go in. She didn't feel the least bit celebratory. The end of her residency felt like the end of one of the most meaningful periods of her life. She'd only had a few shining years where she'd really felt like herself.

But of course, Dr. Dani Martin wasn't who she really was at all. Tomorrow, she'd have to go back to her real life as Princess Danielle-Genevieve in Lorovia. She already had a plane ticket in her purse.

There were too many emotions at war within her, and this was supposed to be an evening of joy. She didn't want her feelings to cloud her classmates' celebration. She stood outside the door, longing to go in, but dreading the inevitable good-byes.

As she stood, an older man stepped out of a taxi and moved beside her. She reeled in surprise.

"Dr. Benson?"

Despite his gruff manner, Dr. Benson had never intimidated Dani as he had her colleagues. Perhaps it was because she was used to dealing with her older relatives, who could be demanding and overbearing. Working with Dr. Benson had sparked Dani's competitive spirit, and she'd been determined to live up to his exact and demanding standards.

His expression was markedly different from its usual scowl. In fact, he looked positively pleased to see her. "I never miss the good-bye party for a residency cohort," he said. "And I had a feeling that if I dropped by, I might see you. I would have hated to miss the chance to say good-bye to one of our brightest residents."

Dani couldn't help flushing with pleasure. It was a compliment she'd worked years to earn. "Sorry I missed rounds last week."

"No need to apologize. I understand that a more urgent matter arose. And that you performed admirably under pressure. No less than I would expect of you, of course."

"Thank you. That means a lot to me."

"But I didn't come over here just to throw compliments at you. I wanted to talk to you about something even more important. Your future."

As a senior attending physician, Dr. Benson was one of the few people at Boston General who knew the truth of Dani's situation.

"Dr. Benson…my future involves going home to Lorovia tomorrow. I was only allowed to pursue a medical education on the condition that I return home to resume my duties immediately afterward."

He nodded. "I know your situation is complicated. But as I've gotten to know you, I've

realized that like all the best physicians, helping people is truly your calling. And there are
so many different ways to help. Not everyone
needs to be a doctor. Certainly, one could argue
that being a princess offers one a wide scope
for helping others. But you, Dr. Martin… I believe that *you* may be called to this profession.
You have what it takes to be a cardiologist, if
you wanted to continue in that direction. Are
you sure that abandoning your career now is the
best path forward?"

She held out her hands. "Even if I wanted to
continue, how could I? All the fellowships are
assigned for this year."

"Not all of them. There are spots at small programs with unusual circumstances. For example, yesterday, Dr. Logan and I were discussing
the Coral Bay Medical Center's fellowship program in cardiology. And he seemed particularly
interested in you."

Cade had asked about her? Even after she'd
told him that it would be impossible for her to
move to the Caribbean?

"Dr. Logan left for St. Camille yesterday. But
he asked me to speak with you one more time,
to let you know that it's a door that's open to
you if you're interested. There's no guarantee on
how long that door will stay open. But it's open

for now. He asked me to give you his number, just in case." He handed Dani a business card.

Even as she took the card, she started to protest once more that she couldn't possibly continue her career in medicine, but he stopped her. "Just take a little while to think about it. And while you're thinking, I want you to have this."

He handed her a pastel-covered envelope, about the size of a greeting card. She opened it, to see a card that looked as though it came from a hospital gift shop.

She read the note scrawled inside.

Dear Dr. Martin,
I can't thank you and all the other doctors enough for being there for me. My own father passed from a heart attack when I was young, but thanks to you, I'll be around to see my own boys grow up. This card is small thanks for what you've done, but I hope you keep it and know that I'm forever grateful.
Thank you for saving my life.
Charlie.

"The man you saved last week is named Charles Brownlow, and he has a wife and two children," said Dr. Benson. "I know that your responsibilities at home are quite serious. But opportunities like the Coral Bay program don't come along often. Frankly, neither do clinicians with the gifts and skill to succeed in such a program. There are lots of ways of helping, Dani. I think being a doctor might be yours."

Dammit. Dani had spent three years maintaining her stoicism under the Benson Glare. But now she felt the tears begin to flow. Dr. Benson had finally made her cry.

"Think about it," he said, giving her a quick pat on the shoulder before he entered the bar.

Dani wiped the tears from her eyes and put both the letter and Cade's business card into her purse. As she did, her fingers touched the plane ticket to Lorovia. She pulled Cade's business card and the plane ticket out and stared at them. She felt as though she held two very different futures in her hands.

Thank you for saving my life.

What could be more important than those words?

She'd made a promise to her family. A princess wasn't supposed to go back on her word. She had obligations to meet and a duty to fulfill.

But wasn't a princess's highest obligation to care for her people?

And as a doctor, she had the skills to care for everyone—not just the Lorovian people, but anyone who needed her help.

What was the point of being a member of the royal family if she couldn't help people?

Thank you for saving my life. She'd thought her future was a settled thing, but those six words placed her on the verge of a decision.

Cade had already left for St. Camille yesterday.

The news left an unexpected emptiness in her heart. He was gone.

Gone, but not entirely out of reach. She had his number.

If she let herself think, she'd never go through with it. She couldn't stop to imagine what her family would say or how they'd react. *Don't think, just do.* She felt the same rush of adrenaline that she'd felt in the ER when she'd jumped into action and started CPR. She pulled her phone from her purse and dialed.

She'd expected it to go straight to voice mail, but to her surprise, he picked up. His "hello" came out deep and resonant, despite the crackling connection.

"Dr. Logan? It's Dani Martin. I'd love to speak more with you about the Coral Bay fellowship program."

CHAPTER TWO

DANI PULLED HER extra pillow over her head, but it did little to block out the thunderstorm that raged just outside her dormitory room at the Coral Bay Medical Center. She glared at the clock on her nightstand. The time glared back at her in neon green digits: four in the morning. She'd gone to bed after midnight, but sleep had been elusive.

She'd been at the medical center for two weeks, yet it felt as though she'd experienced a decade's worth of family conflict. Her spur-of-the-moment decision to continue on with her career had not gone over well with her uncles. She'd known, of course, that they would oppose her choice. Her parents had responded wonderfully, and she was still touched by their words of support. But her father was the ruling queen's youngest son, and as such, he still had to defer to the judgement of his older brothers when it came to broader family matters. It was her older uncles who needed to be convinced, and they were stubborn and used to getting their own way.

It was heart-wrenching for Dani to make a decision that caused so much arguing among her family members. But for the first time in her life, she was willing to fight for what she wanted. Faced with the possibility of losing her medical career forever, she'd realized that she couldn't give up such an important part of her life. Not just for herself, but for the people she could help as well.

Which meant she had no choice but to appeal to her grandmother, the queen.

Dani had always been a little intimidated by her grandmother, who was warm and loving but very strict, especially on matters related to public perception of the royal family. For the most part, the queen left the running of family business to other members of the extended family. But sometimes disagreements arose that were impossible to resolve, and in those cases, her grandmother's word was final.

Dani knew there was a risk in taking her case to her grandmother. If the queen didn't see her side of things, then she'd have to give up her medical career forever. And at first, it did seem as though her grandmother was inclined to agree with her uncles. But everything changed when her grandmother caught the name of the Coral Bay Medical Center.

Apparently, the medical center was more well-known than Dani realized. It was a well-kept secret among the wealthy as a place to obtain discreet health care away from the prying eyes of the paparazzi. In fact, her grandmother revealed, Dani's own grandfather had once been a patient there, and her grandmother credited the doctors there with adding years to his life before he passed.

Her grandmother had spoken to the entire family on Dani's behalf. Perhaps, she'd said, they'd all been too narrow in their idea of what a princess's responsibilities were supposed to be. If Dani had the skills and the ability to save lives as a physician, then she also had a duty to practice those skills. It might be a break from tradition for a royal family member to hold a profession, but weren't those traditions supposed to be for the good of the people? Moreover, her grandmother felt that a debt was owed to Coral Bay, one that could never be repaid. If Dani wanted to practice medicine there, she could do so with the full support of her family.

She would have to continue keeping her royal status a strict secret, for security purposes. And she'd have to continue using the surname Martin. In Boston, the dean of her medical school and a few senior physicians had known Dani's true identity in case Dani ever needed extra security measures or a leave of absence for royal events. But living and working on St. Camille would be different from medical school and residency. There would be no one to hold accountable except herself if her secret got out. The chances of the news spreading, even if she only told one or two people, were far too high. She was, therefore, expressly forbidden to tell anyone of her status, no matter how trustworthy she thought they might be.

Dani agreed to continue concealing her identity without hesitation. It seemed like a small price to pay for the chance to pursue the career she loved.

She was thrilled to finally have her family's consent to work at Coral Bay. But once she arrived on St. Camille, nothing else seemed to go right.

The island's internet had been up and down all week, and she'd been out of contact with everyone. There'd only been one text from Kim—Did you get another chance to feel Dr. BeachBum's muscles yet?

Dr. BeachBum was the nickname Kim had adopted for Cade after hearing Dani's story of how they'd met at Boston General. Dani hadn't been able to get a response through. Due to the unseasonable tropical storms, she hadn't been able to see much of the island's famous white sand beaches and crystal waters. The weather also made it impossible to search for any permanent housing. The Coral Bay Medical Center provided spacious dormitory rooms for all its staff, but they were still rather impersonal, and Dani hoped to find a place of her own as soon as possible.

Her desire to settle in was made more urgent by the loss of her luggage. The medical center had a helicopter pad for flying in patients, but the island was too small for its own airport. Dani had flown by private jet to a larger island and made the last leg of her journey to St. Camille by boat. The ship's captain had seized the chance to travel through a break in the storms. Dani had survived the choppy waters; her luggage, unfortunately, had been loaded at the exact moment an extremely large wave arose, and most of the belongings she'd brought with her were now at the bottom of the sea. It had mostly been clothing and nothing she couldn't live without. But it would have been nice to have some of her own things while she adjusted to a new place.

The medical center staff had given her some spare scrubs to wear until the weather abated and she could shop for clothes. But Dani's frame was petite and they were out of smaller sizes, which meant that Dani had to fold the arms and legs of her scrubs back several times. She felt like a child playing dress-up.

Lightning crackled outside her dormitory window and Dani gave up on any hope of sleep. But it wasn't just the storm that was keeping her awake. She'd risked so much to follow a dream, and now she was far from everyone she'd ever known, living in a room that wasn't hers and wearing clothes that didn't fit.

It was enough to make her wonder if the universe was telling her she should have stuck to being a princess.

It's only temporary, she thought. *I just need time to adjust to the island and to the staff at the medical center.*

But time was a luxury she wasn't sure she had. Because if she had to work with Cade Logan for much longer, she was likely to lose her medical license for assaulting a colleague.

Dani took a deep breath, trying to keep her blood pressure down as Cade came to mind. He was only trying to help. Probably. But if he was also trying to drive her insane, he was doing an excellent job of it.

As the senior fellow in the cardiology program, Cade was responsible for overseeing most of the training that went on at the medical center. Dani understood that Cade took this responsibility seriously. Over the past two weeks, she'd noticed that he was conscientious, attentive and that he listened with genuine concern to his patients. She admired those things about him.

Unfortunately, he was also the biggest micromanager she'd ever worked with.

If she needed to call down to the lab to request a rush on test results, Cade was at her elbow asking why—was there some emergency? And if so, why hadn't she told him? When she was invited to sit in on a surgery, he'd watched her scrub in like a hawk—as though Boston General would have let her go through residency without knowing how to prepare for a surgical procedure. If she got lost in the labyrinth of the hospital's basement and happened to run into him—and she was always running into him; it seemed impossible to turn a corner at the hospital without coming face-to-face with those piercing blue eyes—then he couldn't just help her with directions. He wanted to know where she was going, what she needed and how she'd gotten lost.

And it didn't only affect her. That morning, Dani had been explaining correct procedure for inserting a central line to one of the hospital interns, Matthew. Dani's instinct was to hold back, letting Matthew find his footing on his own and build his confidence. Cade seemed to take a different view—he jumped in almost immediately.

"Keep your hands steady," he'd said to the intern. Dani scowled. As she'd predicted, criticism only served to worsen Matthew's shaking hands. A moment later, Cade jumped in again as Matthew placed a discarded needle tip in the wrong section of the surgical tray.

"Not there. It goes in the top left-hand quadrant of the tray. Keeping your items organized to a standard procedure makes everything run more smoothly." Dani agreed, but thought Cade could have waited until Matthew was finished to provide that feedback. But seconds later, it didn't matter anymore, as Cade took over the procedure and put the central line in himself.

"Better luck next time," he said to Matthew, and then, to Dani, "Make sure you take some time this week to run all the interns through the procedure more thoroughly."

Her blood boiled. Cade turned to leave and she followed him into the hallway.

"Excuse me? Dr. Logan? A quick word?" Her tone was brisk and sharp and he looked up from his chart, confused. His expression was one of total innocence, as though he had no idea why she sounded upset. It was hard to be mad at him when he looked as though he actually cared about what she had to say—but his micromanagement had to stop. She couldn't work like this.

"Is something wrong?"

"Yes, something's wrong! What just happened in there?"

"As far as I can tell, an intern tried to perform a procedure he wasn't ready for, and you seemed hesitant to do it yourself. I took over for the good of the patient."

She gritted her teeth. "First of all, I wasn't *hesitant*. Every intern is nervous the first time they put a central line in. I wanted Matthew to see that he could trust his training to overcome his nerves. But you jumping in with criticism when he'd barely even started did nothing to put him at ease. And taking over the way you did will just make him feel incompetent."

"Hmm. Perhaps we should ask the patient whether he prefers that Matthew feels good about his skills, or that his procedures are performed by qualified physicians."

The suggestion that she hadn't considered the patient's needs was infuriating. "I would have stepped in if the patient were the slightest bit at risk. But training interns is important, too. And now Matthew's going to be jumpy the next time he tries to put a central line in, which is going to be worse for future patients."

To her surprise, Cade's expression softened.

She'd been gearing herself up for a heated argument, but Cade seemed thoughtful. Worry lines appeared on his forehead and she realized that he wasn't about to snap back at her.

"Tell Matthew to hum next time," he said.

"Hum?"

"Yes. Have him and the patient both hum a tune together. There's research indicating that humming during central line placement prevents changes in the patient's central venous pressure, and it'll calm Matthew down, too. It's simple but effective. Have him try it…*after* he's observed the procedure a few more times."

It was a good suggestion, she realized. Why couldn't Cade have simply offered up that idea in the first place instead of jumping all over Matthew and leaving her feeling so unsettled?

"That's a good strategy," she said. "I wish you'd mentioned that to Matthew, instead of taking over."

He smiled at her, one eye closing as he did. "Maybe I was holding back to see if you'd suggest it to him."

And with that, he walked off down the hallway, leaving her even more irritated than she'd been before they'd spoke.

It was Dr. Benson all over again, she realized. Cade was trying to keep her on her toes. She had to stop letting him get inside her head.

Thunder broke outside her window again. Dani decided that since she wasn't sleeping, she might as well do some early morning rounds. It wouldn't hurt to double-check on the patient Matthew had been working with, either. Cade's involvement had made her anxious—that was what always came of micromanagement—and she wanted to make absolutely sure that the case went smoothly.

She slipped out of bed and pulled on her overly large scrubs, determined to set aside the memory of the way Cade's brow had furrowed when she'd questioned him, making his gaze appear even more piercing than usual. She hadn't spent three years withstanding the Benson Glare just to let Cade Logan and his ever-watchful blue eyes drain her confidence. If Cade thought she was going to be fazed by his constant vigilance, he was about to find out that she was made of sterner stuff.

Dani worked her way through the labyrinthine halls of the medical center, nodding at the nurses she encountered through bleary, sleep-deprived eyes. After two weeks, she felt she was beginning to get to know the staff. Aside from Cade, everyone else seemed to be developing trust in her clinical skills.

When she reached her patient's room, she found that Cade was already there.

Why am I not surprised?

He was reviewing the chart at the foot of the patient's bed. Did he not trust her to look after her patients herself? As the senior fellow, Cade should be available for consultation if needed, but there was no need for him to check on each patient personally.

Unless he wasn't checking on each patient, but specifically on *her* patients, because he doubted her competence.

She reminded herself that it was normal for medical teams to take time to work together comfortably. When she'd first started her residency, she and her colleagues had had to learn to stop being competitive with each other so that they could work together, and some of those colleagues had become her closest friends. Maybe this would be the same.

None of her past colleagues, though, had had Cade's twinkling blue eyes or the condescending wink that came along with them. Still, she had to try.

"Ahem." She cleared her throat to alert him to her presence, but a loud thunderclap swallowed her voice. She waited for the noise of the storm to pass, then said loudly, "Excuse me?"

Cade jumped at the sound of her voice. "Surely there's no need to shout, Dr. Martin."

She was glad the lights were still dimmed for the overnight shift; hopefully it made her blush less apparent. "Just wanted to make sure you heard me."

"Well. You certainly accomplished that." He smiled again and, as usual, the quick change in his blue eyes—from steady and focused to bemused—caught her off guard. His eyes were as variable as the ocean; they seemed to pierce her at one moment and mock her the next. It was unsettling—to never know what to expect.

It's no different than the Benson Glare, she reminded herself. *He may be smiling, but he's here because he thinks he needs to check up on your patients. Just stay calm and don't let him see that you're ruffled.*

She returned his smile with a steady gaze, determined to show him that she wasn't in the least bit on the defensive.

"What's got you up so early?" he asked. "Fellowship isn't like residency. You should be taking advantage of having time to get a full night's sleep for the first time in three years."

He wasn't wrong about that. Despite her rocky start at the medical center, one change she'd already felt the full advantage of was the ability to have a regular sleep schedule. Working through sleep deprivation was a normal part of a doctor's training, but the worst of it happened during the residency years. She'd dreaded the weeks when she was scheduled for night shifts and twenty-four hour calls.

"It has been nice to feel well rested for the first time in…" She paused. "Actually, I can't remember the last time I got a full night's sleep. Maybe back in the first week of medical school?"

He laughed. "I felt the same way when I first started fellowship. At first I had so much energy I thought I needed to get my blood work checked, but then I realized that that was just what it felt like to be a normal person going on eight hours of sleep."

It was nice to hear Cade sounding a bit more relaxed. Most of their conversations so far had been discussions about patient care—discussions that left Dani feeling frustrated because Cade so often seemed to give her instructions or information that was already part of her plan. For once, he seemed more interested in connecting with her, rather than correcting her every move.

Still. She didn't need him hovering anxiously over her work or her patients.

"Dr. Logan," she began, wondering how she

could explain this to him in a way he could understand.

"Please. You've been here a couple weeks now. You should call me Cade.

"Cade. Can we go out into the hallway for a moment?"

He accompanied her into the hall. "Why do I get the sense that I'm in trouble?" he asked.

"No one's in trouble. We just need to talk about…this." She waved her arms toward the patient.

He raised his eyebrows, his blue eyes becoming even more clear as he did. "And 'this' refers to what, exactly?"

She tried to find the words to be as diplomatic as possible. "It looks to me as though you're checking up on my patient."

"Is there something wrong with that?"

"Not necessarily. But in case you haven't noticed, *I'm* here to check up on my patient. In fact, ever since I arrived, it seems as though every time I'm about to take care of something, or learn something new or finish something on my own, you're right there to make sure that it gets done."

"I'm the senior fellow, Dr. Martin. Making sure that procedures run smoothly is a big part of my responsibilities."

"Yes, but there's a big difference between

making sure procedures run smoothly and believing that they won't unless you take care of them. Quite frankly, most of the feedback you've given me has all been related to things you would have seen me do anyway, had you waited just a half second longer."

"Can you give me an example?"

"Cade. We're *standing* in an example. When I see you here checking up on my patient, it makes me worry that you don't trust me to have things under control, or to seek you out when I need to."

Cade looked pained for a moment, and Dani worried she'd gone too far. But then he said, "It's not you I don't trust."

"What do you mean?"

He hesitated, as though trying to find his words. "I was a resident here for three years, and a fellow after that. This island, this medical center, means everything to me. It's my intention to stay here on St. Camille permanently. And this is the first year I've had primary responsibility for the training program. I want everything to run smoothly. But what if I can't? What if I miss something? What if something preventable happens on my watch, because I ignored my instincts?"

Dani absorbed what Cade was saying. She'd seen him as confident, capable and in control.

But until this moment, it had never occurred to her that Cade Logan, certified micromanager and control freak, might be *nervous*.

He's not really a control freak. He's just feeling the weight of responsibility, and he's worried about all the things that could go wrong. She could relate to that.

His next words confirmed her thoughts. "I know you're a good physician, Dr. Martin. I read your application, and I've seen you work. I know I should be able to trust you with any patient in the medical center. It's myself I don't trust. What if I'm not ready for this?"

Something about how vulnerable he looked evaporated any lingering frustration she felt. She'd spent the past two weeks wanting to throttle him, but now that he'd finally dropped his air of confidence and admitted his uncertainty, she only wanted to offer reassurance. A shock of blond hair fell over the crease in his forehead, and it was all she could do to resist the urge to push it back and tell him not to worry. Instead, she said, "Well, first of all, you *can* trust your instincts. In fact, you had a good one just now."

His eyes were quizzical. "How so?"

"When you said it was time to be on a first-name basis. Enough of this Dr. Martin business. Call me Dani."

He smiled, and although his eyes had the

same sparkle, somehow it was different; less jarring. The warmth of it enveloped her instead of taking her off guard as it had over the past two weeks.

"I can do that," he said.

She thought for a moment. "I appreciate what you said about trusting my skills. But I think what we need to work as a team is to trust *each other*. And that takes time, but we really haven't known each other for very long. So what do you need from me so that you can trust me?"

He mulled this over. "Transparency," he said, after a moment's thought.

Well, you walked right into that one, she told herself. There was nothing wrong with the idea of transparency, unless one was keeping a fairly large secret. Such as being twelfth in line to a throne.

Cade was warming to the idea. "Yes. Transparency. I think the whole team has got to feel more comfortable with transparency, especially in these early days. And I've got to work on letting go of control. I think the more open and honest we can all be with one another, the more comfortable I'll feel letting go."

Dani gave a weak smile. "Honesty is the best policy."

But how well could she follow that policy? Most of the time, she didn't mind keeping her royal status a secret because she understood the need for discretion and security. But it felt different to hold on to that secret with Cade standing in front of her, openly stating how much he felt the need for honesty and transparency.

It felt different, too, to notice his eyes once again fall along the line of her upper lip, just as they had back in Boston. His eyes rested right where her scar was, tiny and imperceptible to anyone. Almost anyone.

But perhaps not to Cade.

Back in Boston, she'd thought he was simply trying to make note of her features, as anyone might when meeting a new colleague. Except his expression then hadn't exactly felt collegial, just as it didn't now. Something about the way he was looking at her made her lips feel dry. She tried, desperately, to resist the urge to lick them…and failed.

The moment she licked her lips, she saw Cade swallow. There was no mistaking it.

But why on earth should Cade swallow, simply because she'd licked her lips?

You're making far too much of this, she told herself. *People swallow. People lick their lips when they're dry. You're a doctor, you know all about basic bodily functions. Stop acting as though he's looking at you in any particular way.*

But *why* was he looking at her?

Before she could decide how to interpret his intense, piercing expression, the lights went out.

A thunderclap sounded so loudly that Dani jumped. The lights in the hallway went dark and she could barely see Cade's faint outline, let alone his expression.

"The backup generators should come on within the next few seconds," he said. "Don't worry. This happens sometimes during the worst storms."

They stood together in the darkness, waiting.

"Should we be concerned?" Dani asked after a moment.

"Give it just another second," said Cade. Then, when the lights still didn't come back on, he said, "Okay, let's move back toward the wall."

Dani started to move, but as she did, one pant leg of her overly large scrubs came unfurled and she slipped backward with a yelp. Firm arms enveloped her before she hit the floor.

She froze in his embrace for a moment, too embarrassed to move.

"Careful," he said. "Here, I'll hold you up while you get your footing."

He kept his arms around her, turning her toward him as she slowly stood upright. She'd never been close enough to him to notice before, but she could swear he smelled of cinnamon.

She sighed with relief as the lights came back on—but his arms were still around her.

"Are you all right?" he asked.

Now she knew he could see her blush, no matter how dim the lighting was. He was too close to miss it.

"It's just these scrubs," she said. "They're a little long for me, so they're hard to walk in." After a moment, she added, "You can let go." When he seemed reluctant, she added, "Really. I'm perfectly capable of standing." Her exasperation came flooding back. They'd just had an entire conversation in which Cade had acknowledged that he'd been too controlling, and now he was doubting whether she could even stand on her own two feet.

"Of course," he said, moving away from her. "Can I walk you back to your room? Or to the charting station, if you're planning to stay up?"

She rolled her eyes. "There's no need for you to walk me anywhere. It was only a few minutes ago that you were saying some very nice things about backing off and letting go. Here's a chance for you to do just that."

"And you were agreeing to be transparent. But there's something you haven't told me."

Her heart was in her throat. What did he know?

"Those scrubs they gave you. They don't fit you at all, do they? Have you been walking around in oversize scrubs for two weeks? Why didn't you say anything?"

She hesitated. But he was right about transparency. If she couldn't be honest about her one big secret, she could at least try to be forthright about the smaller things. "The admin staff said it might be a few weeks before any new medical supplies come in, especially with the storm delaying shipments."

He shook his head. "The storms can't be helped. But we can put in a rush order for certain things."

"I don't want to be a bother," she began.

"Nonsense. I'll see that it's done." With that, he headed out the door, leaving Dani alone with her mind swirling.

Now that she'd noticed the scent of cinnamon that seemed to cling to Cade, she noticed its aftereffects as well. Traces of cinnamon lingered in the room, faint but clearly there—now that she knew what to look for.

She thought again of the way his gaze had lingered on her lips. Why the hell had he been looking at her like that?

She hadn't had any time to make sense of his expression before she'd almost gone sprawling to the floor.

She could still feel the pressure of Cade's arms against her body. He'd held her for much longer than he'd needed to.

Because he's a control freak who can't let go of anything until he's completely certain that absolutely nothing will go wrong, she thought.

Or...because he hadn't wanted to let go of her.

But that was utter nonsense. She'd fallen in the darkness and Cade had helped her up, the way any civilized human would help another.

The truth hit her harder than the thunderclaps outside the window. She hadn't wanted Cade to let go of *her*. She'd wanted him to continue that embrace for as long as possible. For him to pull her closer with those strong arms, to hold her against the solid chest and the warm, beating heart she'd felt—just for a moment—when he'd had his arms around her. Steadying her.

The thoughts she was having now were far from steady. And far from anything professional. Her mind raced, despite her attempts to bring herself back to reason. She breathed in the last traces of cinnamon in the air and imagined that Cade *hadn't* let go. What would it feel like, for the top of her head to rest in the hollow beneath his chin? For his stubble to graze her forehead? Her skin felt hot as she thought of quite a few other sensations she'd like to have while Cade held her…kissed her…and perhaps did more than kiss her.

Stop. This was pointless. She and Cade worked together, and she couldn't be effective at work if she was distracted by her attraction to a colleague.

Attraction. That's all it was. It couldn't be anything more. For one thing, she had no solid evidence that Cade felt anything for her. She could be completely misinterpreting the way he'd gazed at her. The fact that he'd swallowed when she licked her lips could mean anything. And even if he did feel an attraction, it would probably evaporate the moment he learned the full truth about her.

For a member of the Lorovian royal family, dating didn't exactly lend itself to romance. When she was quite young, her uncle Xavier had sat her down and explained The Rules: Anyone she officially dated would have to sign a nondisclosure agreement. A certain number of public appearances by herself and her consort were required each year. Her consort had to sign legal documents promising not to engage in any public behavior that reflected negatively on the royal family. And that was just for starters.

The rules and regulations were only part of a problem that had plagued Dani since childhood. Even if she hadn't promised to keep her royal status a secret, revealing the truth still wouldn't solve the problem she'd struggled with for most of her life: that of wondering whether people liked her for herself or for her title. And Peter's betrayal, years ago, had left her wary and mistrustful of love.

Which was why the flicker of attraction she'd felt when she'd slipped straight into Cade's arms had taken her by surprise. But now that she was aware of her attraction, she had no intention of allowing that flicker to grow into a flame. She'd come to the Caribbean to learn, to help and to make the most of her medical career while she could. Acting on an attraction was out of the question—especially an attraction that was so fleeting and circumstantial. She was certain that if she ignored her feelings, they would eventually fade.

Her only worry was that maybe glances *did* mean that he was beginning to feel something for her. But even if it was true that he felt something—even if she wasn't just in the throes of wild, sleep-deprived speculation—then he couldn't possibly feel that much for her. They'd only met a few weeks ago; hardly enough time for any strong feelings to develop. If she did her best to communicate a complete lack of interest, then any potential attraction he might feel for her was sure to die down.

She ignored the small pang in her chest that suggested she might not *want* to communicate a complete lack of interest. She'd been a princess long enough to know that what she wanted didn't matter. It was her duty that mattered.

And doing her duty meant doing her best to make sure she didn't reveal her true feelings. That wouldn't be too hard, she thought. She was used to secrets, and she'd become very good at keeping them.

CHAPTER THREE

THE LONG WALK along the beach to Coral Bay was Cade's favorite part of every morning. Cardiology staff were required to live close to the medical center, and on his way to work, weather permitting, he walked along the beach to get to Coral Bay, pacing himself to arrive just as the sun became level with the palm trees.

The solitude of the morning should have been welcome after the recent storms. But Cade found he couldn't enjoy the quiet as he usually did.

His thoughts kept returning to Dani and the conversation they'd had not twenty-four hours ago. He hoped she wasn't regretting her move to St. Camille. She seemed to be adjusting well to the medical center—as far as he could tell, all the staff loved her—but he wanted her to love being there, too. The island needed as many good doctors as it could get, and from what he could tell, the medical center had been extremely lucky to snag Dani right off her residency.

Is it really just about what the island needs, though? He tried to swat the thought away, but it persisted.

He could tell himself that he wanted Dani to fit in for the good of the island. But his reaction during the momentary power outage suggested otherwise.

No—in fact, it had been just before the power outage that his thoughts had started to betray him, despite all his best efforts.

He'd noticed the tiny divot near the right corner of her upper lip when they'd first met. The mark seemed like a scar, perhaps from some childhood accident. She'd have a perfect Cupid's bow if it weren't for that little indentation in the corner. But her mouth wasn't perfect. It was unique, which was even better.

He tried not to think too much about the shape of Dani's mouth, though. Because if he did, then it was only a short step away to start thinking about whether her lips might be soft, which then led to thinking about her skin...which he had no business thinking about at all. Because those weren't the kind of thoughts one had about a colleague. And he very much wanted Dani to continue at Coral Bay as a colleague.

The problem was, he could no longer deny that he wanted other things as well.

When she'd slipped and fallen against him, he'd been exquisitely aware of how close her body was to his. Her hair had brushed against his chin. She'd been wearing it swept back from her face, with loose curls cascading around her shoulders. For an instant, he'd had an insane urge to gather those curls in his hands and let his fingers luxuriate in them. He knew that it was only a fleeting attraction, a kind of momentary madness. But the intensity of his reaction had startled him.

Intense or not, it was still nothing more than an attraction. His feelings would die down soon enough if he ignored them, and it was necessary that he ignore them. He'd sworn off relationships years ago, for reasons that made perfectly good sense at the time and still held true today. Even if he hadn't, getting involved with a co-worker would invite exactly the kinds of complications he preferred to avoid.

There was also no telling how long she'd stay. Island life wasn't for everyone, and if her family situation was as complex as she'd hinted at back in Boston, then he worried she might find it difficult to stay for the three-year duration of her fellowship. He'd seen plenty of doctors arrive in the Caribbean excited to complete their fellowship in a tropical paradise, only to find the distance from home too stressful. If Dani decided to quit, she wouldn't be the first.

She didn't strike him as someone who gave up easily, though. He thought of how her eyes blazed when she'd accused him of being a micromanager. Had he really been that bad? Probably. He knew he had a tendency to seize control when he felt nervous. And there was plenty about Dani that made him nervous. Nothing that had to do with her clinical skills, of course. No, it was more about the wayward tendrils of hair that fell lose about her face and the dark lashes that framed her eyes. He was nervous that he wouldn't be able to stop thinking about her, and he very much needed to.

It was essential that he and Dani be able to get along, as coworkers, because there was a genuine need for her to stay. In addition to providing free care to island residents, Coral Bay Medical Center served a steady stream of wealthy clients who were used to receiving top-notch medical care in luxurious settings. But in order to maintain their reputation, the hospital needed to recruit the most talented staff, and the most talented staff typically wanted to work on the mainland. So no matter how much Cade might notice himself noticing Dani's curly locks or rich brown eyes, he needed to keep such thoughts to himself. If she eventually decided that Coral Bay wasn't for her, it wouldn't be because he'd made things complicated.

Her introduction had already been rocky enough. Until last night, he'd blamed that on the relentless storms. But now, it appeared that he was to blame, too.

He hadn't meant to micromanage Dani's cases. For all his talk of transparency, he'd only given her the partial truth when he'd said he was nervous about overseeing the training program. There was nothing that would have stopped him from hovering over Dani's patient, because that patient was diagnosed with an atrial septal defect. The same diagnosis his brother, Henry, was given, after it was too late to do anything about it.

Henry had passed away at the age of fifteen. If Cade had been a doctor back then, and not merely an eight-year-old boy, maybe he would have noticed that something was wrong. Like the way Henry was always winded after running up the stairs. Or the way Henry sometimes alluded to a tingling in his fingers, as though that happened to everyone. As a cardiologist, Cade could look back and see all the signs of an undiagnosed congenital heart defect.

But no one had noticed the signs in time to help Henry. He'd collapsed after a track meet, and although he was rushed to the hospital, there was nothing anyone could do.

Without Henry to hold the family together, things began to fall apart. Cade's father had never been good at expressing his emotions, and instead of acknowledging his grief, he turned his anger toward the world instead. After their divorce, Cade could tell that his mother was much happier, but he still longed for the family they'd once had.

He escaped his own grief by throwing himself into his schoolwork. He was determined to become a doctor. He might not be able to save Henry, but he could save other families from befalling the same tragedy.

Coming to St. Camille had been an unexpected detour. He had never expected to live in the Caribbean. After graduating medical school, he'd planned to settle down in Boston, where he'd done his training. He'd spent three years with Susan, his medical-school sweetheart, and they planned to marry as soon as he began his internship.

Cade felt as though everything was starting to work out. He had the career he wanted and a life with the woman he loved. A woman who he thought loved him back.

Two days before the wedding, Susan eloped with Cade's best man. Cade did not take it well.

He felt as though everyone he'd ever counted on had let him down. His parents, lost in their grief, had failed to rally to support their remaining child. His best friend, his chosen brother, had betrayed him. And Susan, who he thought was the love of his life, had been lying to him for months. He'd been so busy with his training that he hadn't even noticed they were having problems in their relationship.

And as much as he blamed everyone else, he blamed himself, too. For not seeing what was happening with Susan. Not noticing. Not having any control over the situation, nor any way to stop the helplessness and pain. Just as he hadn't had any control with Henry.

When he'd lost Susan, he stopped attending classes and his ranking fell from first in his class to nearly last. He rallied and took up his studies again just in time to graduate, but by then, his grades had taken irreparable damage. He almost didn't get an internship. After months of languishing in heartbreak and letting his grades decline, there was only one internship program that was willing to consider him. The doctors at the Coral Bay Medical Center were impressed by the passion he showed for medicine. They looked at Cade's history, and the strong recommendations from his professors, and decided they were willing to take a chance on him.

Moving to St. Camille had changed his life, in every way for the better. And if it was far from home, well, there wasn't much at home that he was sad to leave behind. He was better off without relationships in his life—they only led to pain and heartbreak. He found friends among the staff at Coral Bay, and he enjoyed the slower pace of island life.

As he neared the hospital, his phone vibrated. He had a text from his mother: Heard you had some bad storms. Everything ok?

She was the only person he missed, but she'd understood his need to move and they talked frequently.

Aside from his mother, he didn't talk with anyone from his past. He'd anticipated a solitary life on the island, but island life was anything but solitary. Because everyone knew everyone else, there were no secrets. No devastating revelations. He'd had more than enough of those in his life. Secrets always came with sudden, unexpected grief.

After so many complications in his early life, he was determined to spare himself the pain and grief that came with permanent or meaningful attachments. He'd sworn off relationships when he'd moved to the island. He'd had a few brief flings over the years, but nothing more. It was best that way. With no attachment, there could be no loss.

He made a mental note to check on the status of the scrubs Dani needed. Normally such tasks wouldn't be within his purview, but he had a feeling that Dani was the kind of person who wouldn't want to make a fuss over trivial things, and he didn't want her needs to be overlooked. She needed clothes that fit, and those oversize, folded cuffs of her pant legs were a slipping hazard.

Also, the sooner they eliminated the danger of her falling into his arms again, the better.

Her body had been so light in his hands. She'd clung to him, even as she'd insisted she didn't need to.

Of course she clung to you, his rational mind berated him. *That's what people do when they've just slipped. They grab on to whoever's there. It doesn't mean anything.*

And yet. Sometimes he thought he saw her glancing at him, her gaze lingering on him just a moment longer than expected. It probably meant nothing. Or it meant that she was annoyed with him, as she had been last night.

Maybe she'd think better of him if he could back off a little bit. Showed her that he did trust her as a physician and knew that she could handle herself without his constant input. And maybe if he stopped thinking about the way tendrils of her hair came forward to frame her face, he could be more relaxed around her, instead of jumping in with advice to distract himself from the way she made him feel.

And if he ignored his attraction for long enough, it would fade and become a nonissue. It was simply a matter of willpower. This was a good plan. Cade loved plans: they eliminated surprises. He took a look at his schedule for the morning and saw that he and Dani were slated to review some infant screenings. Perfect. He headed to the neonatal care unit, determined to put his willpower to the test.

Dani wasn't sure if the infants on the neonatal care unit today were particularly squirmy, or if all babies were like this. Not one of them seemed interested in holding still long enough for her to wrap the small soft sensor correctly around their hands and feet.

She muttered something under her breath that made Cade give that irritating, half-winking smile of his. "What?" she all but snapped at him.

"You just don't hear a lot of curse words in

the NICU," he replied. "Not that I'm judging. After all, our patients are a little too young to understand most words, let alone the naughty ones."

"I wish I could get them to understand how to hold still." Dani tried adjusting the sensor again, only to have it fall out of place.

Of course, she *would* have to struggle with the procedure while Cade was watching. Dani appreciated that he seemed to be trying to hold back today, watching her do the procedure rather than taking over. But she also had to ignore the traces of cinnamon that wafted from him and the way his blue eyes contributed to the flip-flops her stomach was performing. Neither of those things was assisting with her concentration.

It also didn't help that Cade's shoulders were shaking with laughter. When she looked up at him and glared, he quickly put his hand over his mouth, trying to suppress a smile.

She hadn't worked much with newborns, and she'd never done a pulse oximetry screening before. It was such a routine part of screening for congenital heart disease that she wanted to be familiar with it.

But her tiny patients weren't interested in cooperating. Any hopes she'd had of impressing

Cade had been quickly foiled by babies less than twenty-four hours old.

"Keep trying," Cade said. "You're doing fine."

Dani maneuvered the sensor again and reminded herself that it wasn't Cade's fault that her stomach did gymnastics whenever he smiled.

"Ha! Got it!" The sensor finally stayed in place, and Dani took her reading. She looked at Cade in triumph, but his expression was bemused.

There's something I'm not seeing, she thought. *And he knows and he's just going to enjoy not telling me what it is.*

Her hunch was proven correct moments later as she read the infant's pulse-ox levels. The numbers she was getting didn't match the baby's presentation at all. A baby with oxygen level readings as low as this little infant's should be in significant distress. But the baby in front of her was a hale and hearty newborn with good weight and what she could swear was a wide smile, even though he was technically too young to smile.

"Well?" Cade asked. "What's the verdict?"

Dani shook her head. "It doesn't make any sense. How could his levels be so low?"

"You tell me. Ninety-five to one hundred percent is normal, so below ninety percent means… what?"

Dani really wished that Cade's eyes didn't fix on her quite so intensely every time he asked a question. She started listing the problems out loud: "It could indicate an infection or lung problems. Maybe we should do an echocardiogram."

"Hold on. Let's try something else before we jump to additional tests." Cade scooped the baby out of his bassinet. "This little guy is way too active. Plus, babies are small, so equipment slips around on their bodies. I'll hold him, and we'll see if you get a more accurate reading."

Dani flushed. Of course. She'd been overthinking things. And she'd been trying to rush to a solution in order to get Cade to stop looking at her with that piercing gaze, but she couldn't tell him that.

To add insult to injury, the baby, which had been so fussy with her, instantly became relaxed in Cade's arms.

"There," he said. "This should make things go much more smoothly."

"He calmed down right way," said Dani, her frustration dissipating in the face of the magic of the baby drifting off to sleep. Babies were so vulnerable, yet so trusting. She couldn't remember the last time she'd seen any creature so completely at peace.

"Well, I've had lots of practice," Cade replied.

Dani realized, not for the first time, that she knew next to nothing about Cade's life outside the medical center. "You mean with pediatric patients? Or with children in general?"

"With patients. Kids are great, as long as I can give them back to their parents at the end of the day. I couldn't imagine having one of my own. Having to be responsible for a tiny, vulnerable human, twenty-four hours a day. I don't know how parents handle it."

Dani looked at the way the baby had curled itself against Cade's chest. "I think a lot of it is just instinctual."

"In that case, my instinct is to do whatever I can to heal children, not to raise them."

Dani felt an unexpected sense of loss as Cade spoke. She'd always thought she'd have children of her own one day, even though she couldn't imagine how that would come to pass. Given the difficulties she'd had with dating, it was hard to believe she could ever trust her heart with anyone again, let alone fall in love.

But in light of all the complications of romance, all the obstacles in the way of having a family, she often felt that having children of her own was another dream she should give up. Maybe it could be fulfilling enough to help children heal, rather than raising children of her own. It wasn't what she'd always wanted…but how often did anything in life turn out just the way she wanted it to?

With the baby finally asleep, Dani was able take her readings. "Here. Why don't I hold him so I can slip a sensor around his foot?" she asked. But when she tried to take the baby, he stirred and became squirmy again.

Cade laughed. "Anyone can see that you don't hold babies very often."

She blushed. "How can you tell?"

"You're trying to hold him like he's made of glass. Babies like to feel contained; it's why they're soothed when they're swaddled. Here. Put your arm like this, and don't be afraid to firm up your grip a little. You're not going to break him."

He settled the baby into Dani's arms. She felt more confident, following his advice, even though she was nervous to hold something—*someone*—so delicate.

"Look," Cade whispered. "He's fallen asleep again."

As he leaned toward her, Dani once again caught the notes of cinnamon that seemed to linger about his body. Between his scent and the heat she could feel from his body as he stood close to her, Dani was about at her limit.

Cade's gaze flitted away from the baby and back to her. Once again, he was looking at her with that particular, penetrating gaze. The one that made her lips feel dry.

That did it. A woman could only handle so much.

She placed the baby back in the bassinet and then stood up straight to give the front of her scrubs a brisk brush-off. "Well. Looks like we've got the readings we needed. Turns out his pulse ox was normal after all. Nothing to worry about here."

Cade was quiet. He was still looking at the baby, but his mind seemed far away.

"Cade?"

He shook himself. "I'm so sorry. My mind was somewhere else."

"Where, exactly?"

"It doesn't matter." He gave her a quick smile, but something felt off about it. In the time she'd known him, every time he smiled, his left eye had closed in an involuntary wink. But both eyes had stayed open this time. He was forcing the smile, Dani realized. It wasn't genuine.

She knew she should let the matter drop. If Cade didn't want to talk about something, then it wasn't her business to pry into it.

But what if he needed to talk, but wasn't sure how to start?

"Do you want to grab a coffee from the commissary?" she asked, purely on impulse. Given her attraction to Cade, she should be trying to spend *less* time with him, not more. But she'd been taken aback by his distant expression, just now. Wherever his mind had gone, it didn't seem very pleasant.

"It's not necessary." His voice took on a brusqueness she was beginning to recognize. It was the tone he used whenever a conversation broached personal subjects.

"Are you sure? Because I really don't mind—"

"I said no," he replied curtly.

There was an awkward silence. He had the grace to look shamefaced. "I'm sorry. That was rude."

She shrugged. If Cade didn't want to talk, that was his choice—there was plenty she didn't want to tell him, either. "Not a big deal."

"I only meant that I was busy. I have a full day."

"Okay," said Dani, slowly. "Well, consider it a standing offer, then."

"I will. Another time." And he practically ran from the room.

Great, thought Dani. *He couldn't have left any faster.*

If Cade were that eager to get away from her, then at least she wouldn't have to worry about hiding her attraction from him. But for some reason, the thought didn't make her feel any better. Not even a little bit.

Cade headed down the hallway outside the neonatal care unit, thoroughly frustrated with himself. All Dani had done was invite him to the commissary for a cup of coffee and he'd been cold and abrupt.

He ran his fingers through his hair, mentally running through how things had taken such a sudden downturn. He'd been looking at the baby, his mind lost in thoughts of how different things could have been for his brother Henry if pulse oximetry screening had been a routine part of care when Henry was born. He'd been so wrapped up in thoughts of the past that it had taken him by surprise when Dani jolted him back to the present.

And with that jolt, the immediacy of the moment had hit him with full force. His thoughts had wandered to an emotional place, and with Dani there next to him…his guard had been down. He'd momentarily strayed from the plan of ignoring his attraction to her. Everything had been going so well during the screenings, when they'd both had tasks to focus on. But the moment he'd become lost in his reverie—no, the moment she'd called him back to the present—everything had fallen apart.

He'd realized that he was standing next to a woman he was extremely attracted to, while thinking about some very personal things. And as she'd said his name, he'd found himself acutely aware of her lips again, as well as the way her dark curls settled around her neck and the way her still-oversize scrubs hung about her petite frame.

He knew that he needed to get away from her. He just hadn't planned to make his exit so abruptly. Or so awkwardly. He couldn't imagine what she thought of him now.

He needed to fix this, he realized. Not this week or later today, but immediately. They needed to be on good terms to work together, and he didn't like the idea of Dani being upset with him. He might not want her to suspect his attraction, but he didn't want her to hate him, either.

He went to the commissary but didn't find her there. He bought two coffees and headed back toward the neonatal care unit, hoping he'd see her somewhere along the way.

He didn't have to search for long before he ran into her, almost spilling one of the coffees as he rounded a corner in his haste to find her again.

"It's okay," she said as he tried to brush her with napkins. "You didn't get any on me."

"Good," he said. "I'm glad I ran into you. I wanted to explain about earlier." He held out one of the coffees to her and was relieved when she took it.

She took a sip and smiled. "You know, the coffee here really isn't that bad."

Her nose crinkled just the tiniest bit as she savored the smell from the cup. She pulled her hair back from where it fell around her shoulders so that it all cascaded down her back instead, revealing the delicate outline of her neck. Cade swallowed and took a sip of his coffee, too, just to get his bearings. This was going to be more difficult than he'd thought.

"You see…" He tried to launch into an explanation, and then immediately realized that he had nothing prepared. What could he tell her? The truth? He'd never told anyone at work about Henry.

She motioned toward an empty exam room nearby. "Why don't we go in there? You look like you could use a little more privacy."

He followed her into the exam room, and she shut the door and turned toward him. "What is it, Cade?"

"I just wanted to say that I was sorry—for brushing you off so rudely. You were trying to be friendly, and I want us to be friends, too. But the way I acted was…inexcusable."

She set her coffee down, giving him her full attention. "Apology accepted and appreciated. But is that really all there is? Something seems to be on your mind, and if you want to talk about it, I'm right here."

Her hair had slipped back over her right shoulder, curving inward where her neck met the scoop of her shoulder. His fingers itched to gather her loose brown curls in one hand and reveal the swan-like shape of her neck once again.

Focus, he thought.

"I've been a little distracted, lately," he said. "There's all the responsibility with the training program here, as well as you getting started on the right foot, both at the medical center and on the island."

She nodded and her eyes met his; twin brown pools that he could drown in if he let himself look for long enough. "You've already mentioned that."

"Right," he said, his voice coming out gravelly and low. It was a small room, and she was standing very close to him.

"Cade, in the interest of transparency, why don't you just tell me what's going on?"

She reached out, and Cade realized she was picking a thread from the shoulder of his white coat. He caught her hand. "It's fine," he said. "You don't have to do that."

In spite of himself, in spite of his determination to be an absolute gentleman, he held on to her hand for perhaps a second longer than was proper. Just for a second. It couldn't have been long…and yet, it was long enough that he could take in the softness of her skin. His thumb brushed against the inner curve of her wrist, which was just as soft as the back of her hand, and he knew that same softness would extend to her forearm, and her shoulders and the rest of her, too.

Their eyes met and he swallowed. He let go of her hand, but not before he felt that same electric jolt he'd felt earlier in the neonatal unit.

She took a step closer to him so that there was barely any space between them at all. Her chin was tilted upward, almost begging for him to cup it, and then suddenly he *was* cupping it. He placed his hand against her jawline and tilted her face toward him as he bent to kiss her— tasting citrus lip gloss, a trace of coffee and *her*.

It was over in a second. Or at least, it should have been. He broke away from her, furious with himself and wondering how the hell he could possibly apologize enough for this. He opened his mouth, uncertain of what he could possibly say, but before he could say anything, she was kissing him right back.

Her arms went around his neck and pulled his body close to hers. He held her as his mouth delved into hers, searching again for that indefinable taste that came from her alone. He inhaled the sweetness of her; some soft vanilla scent that mixed with the taste of citrus on her lips, leaving him with the impression of sherbet. He touched the soft locks of her hair, lifting her curls and letting them tumble over his fingers. He was acutely aware of her breasts against him. Her whole body was soft and warm and closer to his than it had ever been before—and yet, not close enough. Not anywhere near close enough.

Cade's pager sounded and they broke apart, meeting each other with startled gazes.

He checked his pager. "It's an emergency."

"Then you should go take care of it."

"But—"

"There's no 'but.' We'll figure this out later. Go!"

She was right. Whatever had just happened between the two of them would have to be addressed later on. He was needed in the cath lab.

As scattered as his thoughts were, his mind registered one thing: Dani had kissed *him*. He'd been the idiot who'd gotten swept up in the moment and kissed her, but then she had kissed him back.

Which meant that she felt something for him, too.

But that made things even worse. Because Cade could handle his own fleeting attraction. Or at least, he'd thought he could, right up until that kiss. But he didn't want Dani to get hurt, and if she became attached to him, she might. Cade had spent six years not allowing himself to get attached to anyone—because getting attached meant you had someone to lose.

He could still taste her lip gloss. He savored it, knowing it was a mistake to do so. He needed to stop things with Dani before they even began. Before either one of them got hurt.

CHAPTER FOUR

THE REST OF the day passed in a blur for Dani. She clung to her training and her professionalism; they were the only two things that allowed her to get through a day filled with patients, lectures and chart reviews after Cade had kissed her.

Kissed her! That was putting it diplomatically. She'd been determined to hide her attraction from Cade, and yet at the first tiny sign of encouragement, she'd practically thrown herself at him. She'd accused him of being a micromanager, of needing to control everything, and then she'd gone and demonstrated that she could barely control herself. She couldn't be more embarrassed.

Somehow, for the first time since she'd arrived at Coral Bay, she'd managed to avoid him for an entire day. She wondered if he was caught up in the cath lab or if he was actively trying to avoid her. They'd have to discuss things eventually, but if he was trying to put off their inevitable awkward conversation, she really couldn't blame him. She wasn't looking forward to it, either.

The more she thought about their kiss, the more she dreaded seeing him again. She couldn't imagine what would be worse: learning that Cade had enthusiastically enjoyed it, or that he felt it had been a huge mistake. Her emotions roiled within her, changing every minute. Wild fantasies of a whirlwind romance with Cade fought with the cold, hard realities of her obligations as a princess and her history of heartbreak.

When she was finally done with her shift, she decided to leave the medical center's campus instead of going to the dormitory. Ever since her arrival, she'd been immersed in work. She longed for a chance to explore this island she'd heard so much about, and with the break in weather, she finally had her chance.

Dani only had to take a few steps outside the medical center's doors before she reached the beach. She felt the tension melt from her shoulders as a light, warm breeze surrounded her. She could just barely taste a hint of salt on her lips, and there was a faint floral scent she couldn't quite identify—hibiscus, or perhaps even orchids, which she knew grew wild on the island. The sun wasn't ready to set yet, though the deepening indigo of the sky promised quite a show in an hour or two. Palm trees swayed on the beach over smooth, flat rocks that jutted out from the white sand.

She made her way toward the rocks and sat down, tucking her knees beneath her chin and wrapping her arms around her legs. *This* was the Caribbean she'd been looking forward to. After a tumultuous start, she could finally start to enjoy the paradise that everyone told her she was living in. She just needed to figure out how she'd managed to mess things up so quickly first.

How had she gone from being so determined to keep her attraction to Cade to herself, to kissing him in an unused exam room?

He said he wanted transparency between us. And he'd gotten what he asked for. After that kiss, he couldn't possibly be in any doubt about how she felt.

She, on the other hand, was mired in confusion. She knew why she'd kissed Cade. She'd done it because she'd lost control. In a split second, she'd made a bad decision, and now she had to learn how to live with it.

But Cade had returned her kiss. In fact, Cade had *initiated* their kiss. Or had he? She was the one who'd stepped close to him just a moment before it happened. Maybe he'd just been leaning forward and she'd drawn the wrong conclusions.

No, that was wishful thinking. This would all be so much easier if Cade *hadn't* welcomed the kiss. But all the evidence suggested their moment together was more than a misunderstanding. She shivered, remembering his fingers buried in her hair; the urgency of his lips against hers. He'd been just as caught up in the moment as she was.

That's all it had been, though: a moment. A second in which they'd both let their guards down and made a mistake. A single moment didn't mean that anything meaningful had happened. A single kiss didn't mean that either of them wanted anything more from one another. It was just one kiss. One really great, exciting, passionate kiss.

She wondered how far things would have gone if his pager hadn't gone off.

It's a good thing you'll never know, she told herself sternly.

But what was she supposed to do now?

More than anything, she wished she could confide in someone. Her phone buzzed in her pocket, and Dani sat up straight. She wrestled her phone from her pocket and rejoiced to see the bars indicating reception in the corner of the screen. For the first time in days, she could use her phone.

She texted Kim immediately: emergency, can you talk now? Miami might be far away, but at least it was in the same time zone as St. Camille.

OMG great to hear from you. What's up? Kim texted back.

Dani hesitated before responding. Maybe she shouldn't put this in writing. But the chances of some tabloid getting ahold of Kim's texts and printing a salacious story were miniscule. And Kim had proven her trustworthiness time and again. Just like Peter, Kim had had chances to sell stories to the tabloids—but Kim had turned them all down. The urge to talk to someone she could trust, someone who knew her better than anyone, overrode any of Dani's worries about security.

I kissed Dr. BeachBum, she texted back.

Her phone rang immediately. Dani swiped to answer the call.

"Tell me every single detail, and don't leave anything out," said Kim.

After Dani finished explaining, Kim said, "Okay. This is all good. This is nothing to stress over. Everything's going to be fine."

"What? How can you say that? Everything will not be fine. I've only been here two weeks and I've already ruined my fellowship."

"Not possible. You can't ruin an entire fellowship with just one kiss." Kim paused. "It was just a kiss, right? You're not leaving out any other salacious details? Because there are absolutely no datable physicians at my oncology fellowship. Everyone here is well into their golden years. So I have to live vicariously through you."

"Kim. Could you please be serious for at least thirty seconds? I need your advice. How am I supposed to talk to him now? How are we supposed to work together?" The thought of even looking at him made her want to cringe with embarrassment.

"You talk to him like a mature adult. You acknowledge that the two of you did indeed have a moment, but now that moment has passed, and you want to keep working together as colleagues regardless of whatever may have happened between you personally."

Kim's voice sounded polished and well rehearsed. Dani had a sudden suspicion. "Kim, why do I get the impression you've had this conversation a few times?"

"Never mind that. We're here to talk about your love life, not mine. And what I want to know is, what do *you* want to happen next?"

Dani paused.

"Dani? Hello?"

"I'm just thinking."

"What's to think about? Do you like him, or not?"

Did she like him? She liked the way he smelled, the way his body moved. She liked the way his lips felt against hers and the waviness of his sun-streaked blond hair. Hair her fingers itched to tousle.

"He's very attractive," she said.

"But not relationship material?"

Dani hesitated. Cade was clearly kind, caring and dedicated to his work. His micromanaging style sometimes made her want to throttle him, but she'd seen enough to learn that even that flaw came from a caring place.

The problem wasn't that she didn't like Cade. The problem was that she could imagine herself liking him quite a lot.

But liking him was out of the question. A fleeting attraction was one thing. Having deeper feelings for someone, getting more attached... that could lead to something more serious over time. And anything serious between her and Cade would be impossible.

"It's not that he isn't relationship material," she told Kim. "It's that I don't think *anyone* would be."

"Because of the princess stuff?"

"Exactly. Even if I could tell him who I really am... I can't put so much obligation on someone else. It's too much to ask. No one would want to be involved in all of that."

"Mmm-hmm. And what about what you want, Princess Danielle-Genevieve?"

Dani sighed. "I'm not sure how much that matters."

"Dani, is being royal really the only issue?"

"What do you mean?"

"Well, I know you had a lot of heartache over what's-his-name. Peter. That guy from college. He caused you a lot of pain. He completely betrayed your trust."

Dani tried to regain her composure. Any mention of Peter always unsettled her. Not because she still had feelings for him, but because even years later, his betrayal still stung. Kim's words were too close to the truth for comfort.

The island's spotty reception was beginning to weaken. "You're breaking up," Dani said, but before she could finish her sentence, the call was disconnected.

What *did* she want now? It was a question that had plagued her for most of her life. Usually, the answer was that what she wanted didn't matter because she had responsibilities.

But that wasn't completely true, she realized. Wasn't she on an island right now, looking at the Caribbean Sea? Wasn't she practicing medicine, just as she'd always wanted?

There were still stipulations. It wasn't permanent, and she had to keep her true identity a secret. But she'd made her dreams come true, at least partway. And partway was better than not at all.

If only it were possible to make things happen partway between herself and Cade. She thought again of Cade's fingers running through her hair. His hands gripping her shoulders. In that moment, she'd known exactly what she wanted. She shivered, remembering the pressure of his hands and the way his mouth had almost devoured hers. He'd wanted her, too. Or at least, he wanted the person he thought she was.

Cade valued transparency. But if she couldn't tell him who she really was, then she had no business allowing herself to even *think* about entering a romantic relationship with him. It was one thing to keep her identity a secret at work. It wasn't an ideal situation, but she did feel she had the right to keep her personal information private from her colleagues. But if she and Cade were to become more than just colleagues, then keeping her secret would be more than just a lack of transparency. It would be a lie of omission.

The sun was meeting the horizon. The sea was still and serene and offered her absolutely no solutions to her problem.

She couldn't tell Cade the truth any more than she could deny her attraction to him. In the past, when she'd revealed her true identity, it had been under very specific circumstances. Kim was her best friend, someone Dani had known for years before she trusted her enough to tell her the truth. She'd only known Cade for a little while. They might be attracted to one another, but they were light-years away from the kind of relationship where she could trust him with her deepest secrets.

The trouble was that being a princess wasn't *just* her deepest secret. It was also an integral part of who she was. But revealing that part of herself was fraught with danger. What if she did decide that Cade was trustworthy enough to know the truth? She'd been through that before, believing that Peter could be trusted to know her true identity, and she'd been betrayed. The fiasco with Peter was a big part of why her family had made her promise not to reveal her identity to anyone else. Her family had never blamed her for Peter's actions—these things happened in royal families—but they did expect her to do everything she could to prevent it from happening again.

But for once, it wasn't her family's fears that consumed her the most. It was her own fear of having her trust broken once more. She couldn't bear the thought of going through heartbreak again with someone else. And if Cade learned the truth about her and didn't react well... Dani knew she was a resilient person, but something deep within her told her that she wasn't ready to experience the emotional roller coaster of trust, love and heartbreak with Cade. Going through it with anyone would hurt, but going through it with Cade might break her.

She pushed the thought away. She was letting her fears get the best of her. There was no reason to start worrying that Cade would break her heart, because she wasn't going to let things get to that point.

She had to tell him, in no uncertain terms, that this could not continue. There was no future for them. She'd have to find a way to explain it that he would believe without revealing her true identity. And she'd need to be convincing, because after the way she'd practically leaped into Cade's arms that morning, he could rightfully claim that she was sending some pretty mixed messages.

She needed to tell him tonight. He was off work, and they could clear the air before their next shift together. Kim was right—no matter what had happened between the two of them personally, they were still colleagues and they should act accordingly. She'd tell him that perhaps they could be friends, and nothing more.

You don't want to be just friends with him, though, a small, knowing part of her whispered.

No, she didn't. Her body didn't lie to her. She knew she wanted Cade. Knew it from the way her breath caught when he'd leaned toward her and the way her heart raced when he'd kissed her.

Those were also the reasons she knew things couldn't go any further.

Partway is better than not at all, she reminded herself. At least if they were friends, she'd still have him in her life. Maybe a friendship with Cade wouldn't be so bad.

Who was she kidding? It would be torture.

But she couldn't see any alternative. If she couldn't tell him the truth, and therefore couldn't be with him, then cutting things off before they got too serious was the responsible thing to do. And if there was one thing a princess was good at, it was meeting her responsibilities.

Cade loved his cottage on St. Camille. Like most houses on the island, it was painted in bright pastels—in his case: yellow with aquamarine shutters. It was happily situated near a beach, which gave him lots of lawn space and an unparalleled view of the ocean from his front yard.

He'd set up a fire pit and two Adirondack chairs in his front lawn, right where the grass met the sand. At the end of the day, there was nothing he liked more than relaxing by the fire, watching the sun set the sky alight before it met the horizon. But today, the calm oceanfront view wasn't bringing the peace it usually did, and he knew why.

He couldn't stop thinking about the kiss he'd shared with Dani. He'd never been so surprised by his own behavior. His plan to hide his attraction hadn't even made it twenty-four hours.

The worst part was that he didn't even feel guilty about it, although he knew he should. He knew perfectly well that he didn't want a relationship. But in that moment, during that kiss… he'd wanted Dani, and once things had gotten started, he hadn't been able to hold back.

He knew he needed to talk to her. The sooner the better. He'd managed to avoid her for most of the day, but he couldn't put their conversation off forever.

Figures dotted the beach: people enjoying the last rays of sunlight. Children played in the light of the setting sun, and a few fishermen began to turn toward home with the day's haul. In the dim light, he could make out another figure walking along the beach, and as it came closer he realized that it was Dani.

He'd known, of course, that he couldn't avoid her forever, especially on an island this small. He'd just hoped he might have an evening alone to figure out what he could possibly say to her.

"Mind if I have a seat?" she said as she approached.

He waved his arm. "Go right ahead. How did you know where I lived?"

"I'm learning that it's remarkably easy to find out anything about anyone on this island. You mentioned that you lived a little south of town, so I walked down to a little group of houses and found out that *was* town, and then a group of children out walking with their pigs told me— and I quote—that this end of the beach is where 'the lonely doctor' lives. So I just walked another four minutes down the path away from the village and found out the lonely doctor was you."

He'd heard some of the island residents call him that. He didn't love the nickname, but he supposed it was accurate.

"What if it had been someone else?"

She snorted. "I thought the risk of anyone else on St. Camille fitting that description was very low."

Fair enough.

There was no need to ask what she was doing here, at his home. He geared himself up, bracing himself to explain…something. But he couldn't fathom how to begin.

"I came to apologize," Dani said. Her words came in a breathless rush, as though she, too, had been struggling with how to start and finally decided to just blurt things out.

"What on earth for?"

She threw her hands up in exasperation. "The kiss, of course! It was a huge mistake. I should never have initiated it."

He knew he should feel relieved that she felt this way. And yet part of him felt disappointed to hear her call their kiss a huge mistake. And why was she apologizing for something *he'd* started? He'd never skirted responsibility for his actions before, and he wasn't going to start now.

"Dani, you have nothing to apologize for. I'm to blame. I was the one who initiated our…*my*… indiscretion."

"No, you weren't. I stepped close to you."

"But I was the one who kissed you."

"Yes, but then I…continued things."

Why was she arguing with him about this? He was fully prepared to take the blame.

Unless she really was trying to spare him pain. He realized that he'd been so focused on protecting her feelings that he hadn't thought about whether she was trying to protect his.

"Let's just agree that it was a mutual mistake," he said. "But to be clear, just because it was a mistake doesn't mean I have any regrets about it."

And he didn't. It may have been a terrible idea that invited far too many complications into his life, but, of course, mistakes were meant to be learned from and not repeated, so he didn't have to regret the taste of her lips or the feeling of his fingers in her hair.

He did, however, regret anything that might cause her pain, and so he quickly added, "I think we also both agree that it shouldn't happen again."

She leaned back in the chair and let out a sigh of relief. Again, he felt a pang of disappointment. The kiss might have been a mistake, but hopefully it hadn't been *bad*.

"I do want you to know that I'm truly sorry if I caused any offence," he said.

"No! I… It was a great kiss, Cade. It's just that…by kissing you, I feel that I sent a message that wasn't true to who I am. Relationships are…complicated for me. And I'm not looking for one right now."

Her words mirrored his own feelings exactly, and he felt a tiny sense of relief for the first time since that morning. His biggest fear had been that she might feel he was leading her on. Offering something more than he could give. But if Dani truly wasn't looking for a relationship, then maybe she, too, had merely been acting on a fleeting attraction. All of this was, indeed, a mistake. A misunderstanding. They could work through it, he was certain.

"As it happens, neither am I," he said.

"Please don't say that just because you're trying to make me feel better. I'm trying to apologize for throwing myself at you. I can't believe I was so unprofessional."

"I'm serious," he said. "You can ask anyone on the island. They call me the lonely doctor for a reason. I haven't had a relationship since—" he stopped, unwilling to face the emotions that came up when he broached the subject of his abruptly cancelled wedding "—since I decided to move to St. Camille," he amended. "I came here to get away from all that."

He knew he was being vague, so he could hardly be surprised that Dani raised a quizzical eyebrow.

"And by 'all that,' you mean…"

"Relationships. The complications they bring. The heartache, the disappointment."

"What about the other aspects of them? Having someone to rely on, someone to care for who cares for you? What about love?"

The sun had dipped below the horizon, and he

couldn't read her expression in the dusky shadows cast by the light from the fire pit.

Love. He couldn't remember the last time he'd heard the word, let alone spoken it aloud. He found that he couldn't even form his mouth around the word now, so he settled for saying, "I found out a long time ago that handing your heart to someone is the easiest way to get it crushed."

Even though he meant every word, he wondered if he was coming across as too cynical. Dani, he thought, was probably someone who believed in things like love and romance. "I suppose that sounds very negative."

"No," she said. "What you're saying doesn't sound negative. It sounds accurate."

In the short time he'd known Dani, she'd struck him as optimistic, hopeful. It was a change to hear her sound so world-weary. Had she been hurt before? Something within his chest roiled at the thought of her being hurt. In his opinion, believing in love was the adult equivalent of believing in Santa Claus, and the sooner one dropped such fantasies, the better. But there was real pain in Dani's voice. If, like him, she'd given up on love, she didn't seem glad of it. She seemed sad.

"I'm guessing relationships haven't been all hearts and roses for you, either," he said gently.

She gave a low chuckle. "Well, maybe the thorny parts of the rose."

"I'm sorry. I didn't realize you were hurting."

"Oh—I wouldn't say hurting. Not anymore. I had a bad relationship—a long time ago—and it taught me some life lessons."

"Such as?"

"That love…love can be a trap. Love creates these expectations, and then when one person doesn't turn out to be who you thought they were, it's absolutely devastating."

"Like there's this whole different side of them that you never knew about all along."

She seemed to shift uncomfortably in her seat. "People are complicated. You can never really know a person all the way. Everyone has… things they need to keep private."

Her voice seemed strained in the darkness, and Cade surmised that this was difficult for her to say. Whoever had hurt her had left a deep wound.

"Secrets can be so destructive," he said. "It's why I can't abide them."

"Oh," she said, her voice small. "Not at all?"

"Well, I agree with you that everyone has a right to keep certain things private. But when it comes to love, secrets only cause pain."

She appeared to be thinking this over. "So for you, if someone were holding back personal information about themselves, something that was really only meant to be known by the closest people in their lives, that would be a deal-breaker?"

"It depends. If I'm one of the closest people in their lives, then yes. I'd want to know that secret eventually. But if it's just a colleague or a casual relationship, then of course I assume there's plenty that people aren't sharing, just as I'm not sharing everything with them. I think the real trouble comes when you start getting close to someone and they're not being honest about what they want or who they are."

Susan had never told him, until the very end, that she wanted completely different things than he did. He'd wanted to stay in Boston; she'd wanted to move close to her family. He'd wanted to travel frequently; she'd wanted to put their money toward a large house. But she'd never spoken about any of this until after she'd betrayed him with his best friend. He'd felt as though he'd never really known her at all.

"Right," she said. "And then you fall in love with the person you think you know, and then they turn out to be someone completely different. And that person you were in love with just evaporates into thin air. They were never real."

"Exactly," he said. "But, for what it's worth, I'm sorry you know how that feels."

She brushed him off. "It was a long time ago. A *very* long time ago." He couldn't tell, in the dim light, if she was blushing, but she sounded a little embarrassed as she said, "I think that may have been part of why I kissed you the way I did."

"What do you mean?"

She was definitely blushing. "It's been a long time since I've had much intimacy with anyone."

Now *his* eyebrows were the ones that raised. "May I ask how long?"

She buried her face in her hands. "I'm too embarrassed to say."

It seemed that they both had something to be embarrassed about. Normally he wouldn't share this kind of information with a colleague. But he and Dani were having an important and necessary heart-to-heart after the events of the morning, and he thought it might make her feel better if he revealed a secret of his own.

"Dani…if it makes you feel any better, it's been four years for me. And then two years before that." Both women had been tourists who were visiting the island for less than forty-eight hours. Both had been very clear about what they wanted and what they didn't.

She took her face out of her hands. "Really?"

"I was telling the truth before. I don't do relationships, and I'm not looking for one."

She mulled this over. "But if it weren't a relationship. If it were just sex and nothing else..."

He shrugged. "Once in a while I have a chance to end the dry spell. But the opportunities are few and far between."

She cocked her head to one side. "Why did you move to St. Camille, Cade?"

"Here's the short version. I had my heart broken, I moved here and now... I do my best not to get my heart broken again."

"Which means not getting close to anyone."

"Exactly. So you see, you're not the only one who has something to apologize for. I kissed you, knowing full well that things wouldn't go anywhere after that. It was unconscionable of me."

"Okay, but if you felt it was such an unconscionable thing to do, then why do it at all?"

He paused. All the reasons he *had* kissed her were hitting him full force as she sat next to him in the dusk. The angle at which her hair fell against her neck, begging him to stroke it, to cup her cheek and tilt her face toward his. Her lips were gently parted. He wondered if they still tasted like citrus, or if she hadn't reapplied her lip balm since that morning.

He mustered every ounce of restraint within his body. "It was just a mistake."

"Cade. Forgetting a patient's name is a mistake. Wearing mismatched socks is a mistake. What was this?"

He couldn't hide it anymore. "It was a momentary lapse in judgement. I let my attraction get the better of me."

Her ears perked up. "Attraction?"

He shook his head. "That was the wrong word."

"Okay, then what's the right word?"

He searched for a moment, then admitted, "Attraction."

So much for his plan to hide his feelings. It was all out there now, under the stars. He hoped he hadn't made Dani feel uncomfortable.

"Six years," she said.

"What?"

"That's how long it's been for me. Six years. Do you realize that between the two of us, that adds up to a decade without physical intimacy?"

"When you put it like that, it does sound like one hell of a dry spell." He was trying to keep his tone light, but the truth was, all this talk of celibacy was doing little to diffuse his attraction. He was acutely aware of Dani's body near his in the darkness. It was more than the warmth of the nearby fire that made his face flush.

She turned her face toward him, and he was surprised at her agonized expression. "Cade, I know this might sound crazy. But I've been doing a lot of reckless things lately—moving here, starting this fellowship. I told you back in Boston that I have a lot of family expectations. But I'm ready to make some choices for myself. And you were brave enough to say it, so I will, too—I'm attracted to you as well. That's why I kissed you this morning. Because I couldn't help myself. And I felt so embarrassed about that, but now, after talking to you, I think... I think that's why you kissed me, too."

He swallowed. "But you aren't looking for anything serious."

"Absolutely not. And neither are you."

"So...where does that leave us?" he asked.

She sighed. "Right where we started. We're colleagues, friends. Anything between us would be incredibly complicated."

She paused, and they sat in silence for a moment. Then she added, "Unless we both decided that it wouldn't be complicated."

"What do you mean?"

"I mean that it's been ten years between the two of us. Ten years of unwanted celibacy. We have an opportunity here to help each other out. All we'd have to do is remove romance, and love, from the equation."

He thought he was beginning to understand, but he wanted to be sure. "How would that work?"

"All it would take is one night together. One night to get this out of our systems and move on."

Part of him couldn't believe she was saying this. The other part of him was screaming at him not to let this opportunity go. But if she really was suggesting what he thought she was suggesting, he needed to be absolutely certain they were on the same page.

"One night. And then in the morning?"

"We go on together as friends and colleagues. That's it. No ongoing relationship, no expectations."

Well, he could understand the appeal of that. But what about her? He couldn't risk hurting her feelings, no matter what she said. "Dani. Are you sure that's what you want?"

"Ten years, Cade. Six for me. Four for you. In one night, we can end something that's been going on for years for both of us, and prevent weeks of awkwardness while we wait for whatever this is between us to die down. If it dies down."

He hesitated. His body ached to finish what they'd started with their kiss that morning. But he'd never, in his wildest dreams, expected Dani to find him on the beach and propose something like this. He believed he could protect his own heart, but what about hers? He couldn't bear to think of Dani being heartbroken and him being the cause of it. How could he know she wouldn't regret it?

She stood up, and suddenly he realized she had taken his hesitation for refusal. "This was silly," she said. "I never should have brought it up. Let's not mention it again. I'll see you at work." She stepped away from him, toward the beach.

"Dani, wait!" He jumped after her and reached for her wrist. She turned to face him, and he saw her eyes were blurred with tears. "You're absolutely sure? No expectations? No additional involvement or commitment to each other? Complete freedom from obligations? That's all you want?"

"Cade, you have no idea. It's all I've ever wanted."

He pulled her to him, and found that the taste of her citrus lip balm was indeed still there, strong and sweet as ever.

CHAPTER FIVE

DANI FELT AS though her body was melting into Cade's. The moment he'd stopped her on the beach, the moment he'd made it clear that he considered her insane proposal to be an actual, real possibility, she'd given up trying to hold back. He'd pulled her to him and met her lips with a kiss that made her drop all the restraint and professionalism she'd been doing her best to maintain since she'd arrived on St. Camille.

No. If she were honest with herself, she'd been hiding from her own feelings since they'd met in Boston.

But there was nowhere to hide now as Cade kissed her on the beach with an urgency that matched her own. The cool of the night air hit the back of her neck as he gathered her curls in his fingers, while the heat of his body sent a warmth spreading through hers.

He leaned his forehead against hers, looking straight into her eyes.

"My house is right over there," he said.

"Then I guess all we have left to do is go inside." She couldn't believe how bold she sounded. All her life, she'd been everything a princess should be: biddable, demure, responsible. But from the moment she met Cade, something had changed. Suddenly she was chasing her own dreams. And apparently, now that she'd gotten a taste of it, she wasn't going to stop.

Her recklessness shocked her. But she wasn't afraid of it. She recalled the pressure of Cade's lips against hers. Maybe it was a mistake. But if the two of them had just one night together, she wasn't going to end it with any regrets.

Cade put his arm around her and walked her through his front door. The beach had been fairly quiet, but the second they were inside, with the guarantee of privacy, she found herself overcome, not just with wanting but with *need*. She barely caught a glimpse of his home before she turned her face to his again. Her arms wrapped around his neck.

He put one arm around her waist and pulled her close while his other hand traced her jaw and tilted her face upward to meet her lips with his. She parted her lips for him and his tongue entered, exploring her mouth with a slow kiss that flared the fire of deeper sensations within her body.

His hands stroked her shoulders, then fell to her breasts. He filled her senses. She was consumed with the smell of cinnamon, sweat and *him*. Her skin felt hot where he stroked her, and the taste of his lips made her insatiable. She already had her arms entwined around him, and as she leaned back against his front door, she was unable to stop herself from entwining her legs around him, too. After years of meeting her responsibilities, years of denying her own needs, she was finally getting something she wanted. She had neither the will nor the inclination to restrain herself. She wrapped her legs around his body, and he slipped his hands beneath her bottom for support. He turned and set her down on what she realized must be his kitchen table, but she was too preoccupied to take in the decor.

She sat on the table with her legs on either side of him. One of his hands was in her hair, while another reached under the skirt of her dress to trace her leg. He moved her skirt aside and pulled her bare thigh closer to his body as his mouth once again sought entry to hers. Her yearning deepened as his hand slid higher up her thigh and found the nook of her hip. A thin layer of lace was all that separated her from his touch, and now his fingers slid beneath that layer, and she shivered as he tantalized her with steady strokes.

She wanted him closer to her, though it seemed he could never be close enough. She pulled off his black T-shirt and took a moment to appreciate that his body was everything that had been promised: taut, muscular and lean. Her hands went to his belt buckle and, after a moment or two, with very little effort, he stood naked before her.

But she didn't have long to look at him, because he moved close again to kiss her neck, working his way down her clavicle, and then to the side of her breast.

His hand went to the back of her neck, where she'd tied the knot of her halter-top dress.

"Do you know what I love about these types of dresses?" he murmured into her skin. "They're like a magician's trick. All you have to do is know how to undo the knot." His hands worked at the knot she'd tied, and all at once, the dress fell around her with the soft *whoosh* of crumpled fabric.

She suddenly felt nervous. She was wearing nothing but her panties. A bra wouldn't have worked with the halter dress. Unconsciously, she lifted her hands to cover her breasts.

He caught her wrists. "Please. Just let me look a moment. Don't hide yourself from me."

She relaxed. Or at least, she relaxed as much as she could under his piercing gaze. His eyes were the cerulean blue of the ocean, and they washed over her now. He reached for her and pressed his lips against her neck. He traced his finger down her shoulder, and then her breast. She felt her nipples rise at his touch.

"I don't think I'm going to make it to the bedroom," he murmured.

"Neither do I." She glanced over to where her purse had been flung onto a chair. "Let me just grab a condom from my purse." She gave silent thanks to Kim for having put the condom there years ago, despite her own protestations that the chances of her ever needing such a thing were extremely slim. Dani hadn't believed she'd ever need it, but she'd never bothered to take it out of her purse, either. She'd jokingly thought of it as her wishful thinking condom.

Well, all of her wishes were coming true now.

"Let's not wait for the bedroom," she said, handing him the foil packet. "Both of us have been waiting long enough."

He gave her that half-winking smile of his and put the condom on. And then laid her down on the floor.

She felt his hands reach to strip her panties off. And then his body was once again melding into hers. He entered her in one smooth, slow motion, and she felt her body adjust to his.

It had been so long. Their motion felt like a dance her body had been awaiting for years. Her hips swung as though to a familiar tune, but somehow, everything felt brand-new.

Her hands clutched his arms as they swayed together, and then fell over the precipice together. She felt his body jerk and heard him say something with his face buried in her hair. It was her name, she realized.

He slipped out of her, exhausted, and lay on his back next to her. He had just enough energy to pull her body against his. She lay with her face pressed against his chest, one arm draped over his chest, and one of her legs draped over one of his.

She couldn't believe what she'd just done. None of it was typical for her at all. The spontaneous sex. The fact that she'd been so forward, so aggressive, in giving herself to him. The whole idea of a one-night stand with no expectation of a relationship, and with a coworker, no less. It was all so *unlike* her.

And yet, at that moment, she felt more like herself than she had in years.

Cade blinked his eyes against the bright morning sun streaming through his shutters. Last night, after their initial unrestrained episode on the kitchen floor, they had eventually made it to his bedroom. It had been a close call, with numerous opportunities for both of them to distract one another along the way, but they'd made it.

The morning air was cool and he tried to pull his bedsheets closer around him, only to feel a resisting tug.

Dani was still asleep, the majority of his sheets wrapped around her, leaving him only one relatively small corner.

Ah. So she was a blanket thief. Somehow, he wasn't surprised. After last night, he was forced to admit that his initial impression of Dani—that she was quiet and didn't like to be a bother—was mistaken. Last night, she'd shown him that she was the kind of woman who took what she wanted—in all the best possible ways.

Blankets, though, were up for negotiation.

He lifted the sheet and pulled it toward himself, revealing her naked body underneath.

She stirred as the cool air hit her. "Hey. I was using that."

He stretched the sheet so that it covered both of them, and then moved closer to her so he could warm her with the heat of his body. "Better?"

She smiled. "Mmm. Much."

He held her like that for a while, still reveling in the satisfaction of the night before.

It should have been the perfect morning, with the sun streaming into his room and Dani in his bed. But he couldn't relax completely. Guilt nagged at him.

Dani had been very clear last night that she was completely open to a one-night stand between the two of them. Hell, it had been her idea. And in the heat of the moment, he'd been perfectly willing to convince himself that they could enjoy a single night of physical intimacy, and then return to being just coworkers in the morning.

But now that the moment had arrived to put their intentions to the test, he wasn't certain if things would play out exactly as planned.

Now, as he held her, his discomfort grew. He felt the familiar urge to *do* something about it, but he didn't know what. Dani was dozing peacefully; he didn't want to disturb her with questions about their arrangement.

Just take it one step at a time, he thought. Dani was sleeping; there was no need to wake her. And it wouldn't be productive to worry— right now—about what things would be like later today at work. They'd cross each bridge as they came to it.

Breakfast. That's something you can take

care of right now. French toast might not solve every problem, but it would give him something to do with his hands and something to focus on besides his worries.

He kissed the top of Dani's head and said, "I'll be in the kitchen. Come in when you're ready."

He made coffee and sliced some good brioche bread. He'd just put the first two slices on the stove when Dani padded into the kitchen, his bathrobe wrapped around her.

"Is that coffee I smell?"

He nodded toward the coffeemaker. "I have cream and sugar in the fridge, and the French toast will be ready in five minutes."

"My hero." She poured coffee into the mug he'd set out for her and lifted it to her nose, savoring the scent.

He handed her a plate of French toast, and they sat at his kitchen table together. She took a few bites and then stopped.

"Something wrong?" he asked. "I can put it on for a few more minutes if it isn't cooked well enough."

"No, it's perfect."

"Then what's wrong?"

She hesitated and then said, "We both got pretty carried away last night."

A jolt of worry shot through him. "I hope there aren't any regrets."

"Not at all," she replied, and his relief was palpable as she gave a small, reminiscent smile over her coffee. "Last night was… Let's just say last night is going to remain a lovely memory."

"And what about the future?"

"Well…this is it, right? We agreed. Just one night."

"Right. I just wanted to make sure we were still on the same page."

She gave him an irked expression. "Cade. Why are you still asking me about this? I told you last night—I didn't want any attachments or expectations. Isn't that what you said you wanted, too?"

"Yes. I just wanted to make sure you don't get hurt."

"Cade. That's sweet of you to care, but please rest assured that I am perfectly capable of protecting my own feelings."

"I just worry that—"

"Oh, my God!" For a moment he was afraid that she was upset, but he saw she was laughing as she set her coffee cup down. "You're doing it again. You're worrying about my feelings, so you're micromanaging and trying to be in control."

He was about to argue, but then realized that

that was, in fact, exactly what he was doing. "Sorry," he said. "Force of habit."

"See? If this were anything more than a one-night stand, I might be upset. But since it's not, I can brush this off as a charming personality quirk that you're working to change. Seriously, Cade. Let me worry about my feelings, and you can worry about yours. That's what friends and colleagues do, right? And that's what we are."

"Of course," he said. "So at work, we'll just… keep things professional."

"Professional. And secret," she said. Suddenly, her face was stricken. "But you hate secrets. I didn't think of that before…"

"This can be our secret," he said quickly. "It's our business. There's no reason to tell anyone else. It's not really about secrecy, but about privacy."

He saw her shoulders drop with relief. "Thank you," she said.

"Of course." It had never occurred to him to breathe a word about their tryst to anyone else, but it never hurt to officially agree on these kinds of things. He was glad that he and Dani seemed to feel the same way.

They were so compatible, he thought. For example, they were both early risers. There were still three hours left before either of them needed to be at work.

He noticed that Dani was also glancing at the clock, and then back at him, as she sipped her coffee.

"You know," he said. "It occurs to me that we have quite a window of time this morning before we need to go in to work and put on our professional game faces."

She set her coffee cup down and turned to him, her eyes sparkling with mischief. "What exactly are you suggesting?"

"That maybe our night together doesn't need to end until we walk out that door. Which doesn't need to be for another two and a half hours."

"Hmm." She licked some of the syrup from the French toast from her lips. "Whatever could we do to fill the time?"

He moved toward her and slipped off his robe. "I have a feeling I can think of something."

And he did.

Several days later, Cade's face was drawn with concentration as he monitored the patient's vitals. Taking a patient off of a heart-lung machine was always an unpredictable process, but so far, this was one of the smoothest cases he'd ever seen.

He had to give credit to the team in the room. The nurses and the perfusionist at Coral Bay were all top-notch, and it helped immensely to have Dani on the team as well. The more he worked with her, the more he noticed the difference her presence made. Not only did she fit in seamlessly with the rest of the staff, but she also had a way of bringing them together around her. He'd always been proud of the way the team at Coral Bay responded to a crisis, but with Dani there, he noticed a shift in tone. It was as though the team wasn't just reacting, but responding. Rising to a challenge instead of scrambling to deal with an emergency.

The ascending aorta they'd just replaced was no exception. Unexpected difficulties inevitably arose in this type of surgery. The patient had been put into circulatory arrest, his body cooled to less than twenty degrees Celsius. The team had sailed through the procedure with ease, but now they faced the complicated process of weaning the patient off the heart-lung machine. No two patients ever responded the same way; it was always a matter of trial and error to see what worked and what didn't.

As nerve-racking as these procedures could be, Cade relished the opportunity. He felt as though these situations called for what he did best. Preparation. Control. Offering direction and suggestions. He took pride in being someone who knew what to do in a crisis, and he felt his team drew reassurance from that.

The team pushed O-negative blood into the patient, gradually warming his body. As minutes passed, Cade began mentally ticking off the plans for unexpected changes. Things were proceeding so well that it was making him uneasy.

"Medication ready?" he asked one of the nurses.

"Syringe is in the tray if we need it," she reassured him.

"Dr. Martin, defibrillator ready to go?"

"The moment we need it," she replied.

"Good. I know things are going well, but we still need to be ready for anything. A case like this can take a turn for the worse fast if we're not ready with the right intervention at the right time."

The team *was* doing well, though, and so was the patient. Cade hadn't missed the flash of annoyance that crossed Dani's face when he'd asked if she was ready with the defibrillator. And in all fairness, that look of annoyance might have been inappropriate if he'd asked her once…but he'd asked her three times already. He hoped it was only three. The rest of the team was used to his obsession with checking every detail, but Dani was new… She might assume that once again, he was micromanaging the situation.

Perhaps he *was* micromanaging. But how else was he supposed to alleviate his worry that he might have missed something? He knew, deep down, that his patient was in good hands and that his team would do everything they could to the best of their ability. But what if *he* made a mistake? What if he overlooked something, the way Henry's doctors had overlooked the signs of his condition?

You've got this, he thought. He'd double- and triple-checked everything. And the patient's response to treatment so far had been very encouraging. He let his shoulders relax by a fraction of an inch.

At that moment, the heart monitor gave an erratic blip.

"A-fib," he called out. "Dani, get the—"

But Dani already had the defibrillator paddles at the ready. She gave the patient a single shock to the heart.

Everyone in the room held their breath. Dani charged the paddles for another shock—and the heart monitor began a steady, rhythmic beep.

Cade couldn't help the smile that burst over his face as a cheer filled the room. The patient was breathing on his own. His heart was beating on its own. A patient who could have been facing death would now have a new lease on life. It was a feeling that never got old.

He looked across the room and locked eyes with Dani. She, too, was flush with excitement. He could tell she shared that same feeling of awe at how a patient so close to death could suddenly have their whole life in front of them.

He wanted to share that moment, that excitement, with her. But he forced himself to tear his eyes away.

Over the past few days, he'd done the best he could to be cordial and professional when they worked together. He was finding it to be more difficult than he'd expected.

It was only supposed to be one night, he told himself fiercely. *One night to get our attraction out of our systems. And then we move on.*

But the "moving on" part wasn't happening as quickly as he'd wanted it to. Despite his efforts not to think about it, his night with Dani was burned into his brain. He'd thought that once he'd finished what they started with that kiss, he'd be over her. That was hardly the case. Whenever he had a free moment, he found himself thinking about her. The way she smelled, the way her body had felt in his hands, the way her bare skin had melted against his.

So he did his best to make sure he didn't have many free moments. He was back to filling his time up with as many tasks as possible and avoiding Dani whenever he could. Which wasn't often, because they had to work together so closely.

The team filed out of the room, exchanging high fives. He suddenly found himself face-to-face with Dani. And then, just as suddenly, he was alone with her for the first time in days, as the rest of the team spilled into the hallway and dispersed.

Her eyes were still alight with excitement. "Is it always like that?" she asked, breathlessly.

He had to smile at that. No matter how conflicted his feelings toward Dani might be, it was impossible not to feel inspired by her love of medicine.

"It's different every time. That was an unusually smooth procedure—but as you saw, anytime you take a patient off of a heart-lung machine, there are going to be complications. It's like a puzzle, figuring out what the patient needs and how each body responds differently."

"It was a miracle," she breathed.

He remembered that when they'd first met, she'd told him she loved medicine because it was full of miracles. "I couldn't agree more."

"Can I ask you some questions about the dose of inotropic drugs we used?"

"Sure. I have some medical journal articles

in my office you can borrow." The second he made the offer, he realized that they'd have to go to his office to get them. Which would mean a few more moments alone with her.

But he couldn't rescind the offer now. He'd promised that nothing would change between them, and there was no way for him to backtrack without looking awkward.

Her eyes were still glowing with the thrill of success. He swallowed. His office was only a short walk down the hall. It would be a matter of seconds to reach into his filing cabinet and give the articles to her to read on her own.

"So, uh, let's just head over to my office and get them," he said.

They walked to his office in silence. Cade's mind was screaming at him to say something, but his mind was completely blank. All he could think of was how to get out of being alone with Dani as quickly as possible, because the more time he spent with her, the more preoccupied he became with thoughts he needed to leave behind.

One night together. That's all it was. She agreed. You agreed. So leave it in the past where it belongs.

After what seemed like an eternity, they arrived at Cade's office. He handed her the journal articles and then didn't let go. They both stood there, holding on to either end of the paper. Cade knew he was being foolish. He needed to get himself under control before he did something completely stupid.

But it was too late. Dani pulled the articles toward her, but instead of letting go—as any sane person would have—he maintained his grip on the paper. Which meant that Dani pulled *him* toward her, too. He hadn't meant for that to happen; he just wasn't thinking clearly. And he *definitely* wasn't thinking clearly when he bent his head down, and she pushed herself up on her toes and kissed him.

He knew he should stop. He certainly shouldn't wrap his arms around her waist and pull her close as he did. But the flavor that lingered on her lips tantalized him, and the light vanilla scent of her threatened to block out everything else.

He was in danger of getting lost in that kiss when she broke away from him.

"I'm so sorry," she said. "I can't believe I just did that. After all we talked about—everything we agreed upon. I don't know what's wrong with me."

With her? What about him? Despite all his good intentions, they'd ended up exactly where neither of them wanted to be.

Well, that wasn't entirely true. It wasn't that they didn't *want* to be there, but that they *shouldn't* be there. Because neither of them wanted a relationship, and if they weren't careful, they were going to end up getting attached.

Unless they made sure they didn't get attached.

An idea was beginning to worm its way into his head.

"I shouldn't be leading you on like this," Dani was saying. "There's absolutely no way there can be anything more between us, and here I am sending you mixed messages once again. I promise to keep this under control. It won't happen again. We can be coworkers and nothing more. I swear."

Her words made Cade even more certain of his next step. Dani clearly believed that *she* was leading him on, that *her* difficulties were preventing the two of them from having a relationship. He was starting to learn that that was who Dani was. Unless someone spelled it out for her, she would assume that everything was her fault. And he was determined to prove to her that it wasn't.

"Dani," he said gently, "I don't think that's going to work."

Her eyes widened. "It has to work," she protested. "I just need to try harder. Be more professional."

He took her hand. "That's not quite what I meant. We've both been trying hard to be professional, but it's not working. We keep ending up in situations like this. I think maybe we need to keep trying, but in a slightly different direction than we have been."

"What do you mean, a different direction?"

"I think we need to make a modification to our original plan. Originally, we thought that one night would be enough for both of us to work out our mutual attraction to one another. But I think we need more."

"But we agreed not to have a relationship."

"This wouldn't be a relationship. This would be a purely physical arrangement, with no strings attached. No expectations of anything more."

"So an extension of last night, essentially."

"Exactly."

She mulled this over. "I suppose we would need to have some ground rules, to make sure neither of us gets hurt."

Now she was speaking his language. Cade valued rules, order and control. It kept things safe. Unpredictability might be fun, but it was also dangerous.

"For example," she continued, "What if you get to a point where you do want something more than what I can offer, and you meet someone who wants the same things? And perhaps we should discuss shelf life, too. How long is this going to go on?"

"How about, it goes on as long as we're both having fun? If it starts becoming stressful, or if it stops being fun, perhaps we should stop. Or at least agree to take a moment to reevaluate where we stand."

"But what about the other part? About you meeting someone else."

"Dani." He looked at her with as much conviction as he could summon. "There is absolutely no chance of me meeting someone else and wanting anything more than this with them."

"You say that now, but—"

"No. I need to explain."

He paused, trying to find the right words. It had been so long since he'd talked about his reasons for avoiding relationships that he wasn't sure where to start. "There's a reason I've lived on an island for six years. I'm not looking for any strong attachments. I was engaged to be married once. Right at the end of medical school. She left me for my best friend, just a few days before the wedding."

Dani winced. "That's awful. But to swear off relationships entirely—all because of that? Wouldn't you someday want a second chance at love? Or if you don't believe in love, then maybe…happiness?"

He hesitated. It had been years since he'd talked about Henry with anyone. Years since he'd had to explain exactly why getting close to anyone meant reactivating all the old worries about loss and heartbreak.

But he was spared from trying to find a way to talk about Henry when Dani put her hand on his arm. "You know what? You don't have to explain. I shouldn't even have asked. Those kinds of questions are meant for relationships. And we're discussing something very different."

He was relieved that she was willing to let the matter drop. Although, just to be on the safe side, he asked, "And what about you? What if you meet someone?"

"I can absolutely guarantee that's not going to happen." At the look of consternation on his face, she said, "Okay. How about this? We both agree that we're entering into this arrangement for as long as it's completely fun and stress-free for both of us. If, at any time, either of us wants to end the arrangement, whether it's because we've met someone, or we just don't want to continue—for *any reason at all*—then we agree that it's over."

"Fair enough."

"And we should continue keeping it a secret from our coworkers as well."

"We can try. But it's very difficult to keep a secret on St. Camille."

"All the same, I'd like to try keeping it private for as long as we can."

"Fine." He smiled. "If it's that important to you, then we can keep it to ourselves."

"Thanks. I appreciate it."

"So…see you at my place tonight?"

She gave him a wink as she went out the door. "Count on it."

CHAPTER SIX

DANI SAT FACING the ocean, luxuriating in one of the biggest perks of working as a doctor in the Caribbean: the warmth of sand against the soles of her bare feet. The medical center's cardiac wing boasted a courtyard that led straight out to the beach, and Dani loved taking her midmorning coffee there and relaxing by the water. She usually had a short break before she began her afternoon rounds, which gave her just enough time to decompress from her morning cases.

She'd never been able to relax like this back in Boston, but at Coral Bay, breaks were actively encouraged—and Dani was starting to enjoy them. Today, she'd removed her shoes and worked her feet into the dry, sun-warmed sand, reveling in the sensation of each grain slipping between her toes. The courtyard's palm trees swayed gently above her. The aroma from her coffee wafted toward her nostrils, and she felt the lingering stress from work melt away as her feet absorbed the heat of the sand and the azure expanse of the ocean that stretched before her.

Even though Dani's fellowship kept her busy, she'd never felt so relaxed in her life. Part of that was simply because life in the Caribbean was beginning to have a positive effect on her. The slower pace of island life, the beauty that surrounded her and the sense of community that came with living in such close proximity to her colleagues and patients were all affecting her in positive ways.

But the biggest change that impacted her was the arrangement between her and Cade. Six weeks had passed since they'd begun their experiment in being together without being emotionally involved. They'd spent more time in one another's bedrooms, had clandestine meetings at work and exchanged meaningful glances when they were certain no one else was looking.

As far as she could tell, no one at work suspected a thing between the two of them. For once, she was able to enjoy a connection with someone else that was about what she wanted, rather than expectations or obligations. And Cade continued to surprise her every day. He was an excellent cook, and he proved to be very helpful in her ongoing search for living quarters because he knew so much about the island and its residents. For someone who claimed that he preferred to be alone, he certainly knew plenty of people. He was always introducing her to groups of island children and shopkeepers in town.

She felt a whirring in one pocket of her white coat and saw that Kim was inviting her for a video chat.

Dani hesitated. Internet connection on the island was so spotty that she hadn't spoken to Kim for weeks. Not since they'd discussed having a calm, professional conversation with Cade about how the two of them weren't going to kiss again. And now things had gone in a very different direction. What if Kim was disappointed in her?

But Kim had never judged her before. Dani decided that if the subject of Cade came up, she'd tell her friend all about it. Kim had never revealed any of her secrets. Not telling her would be unfair and an insult to her friend's loyalty.

Who knows, she thought. *Maybe it won't even come up. I shouldn't assume she's been thinking about it. Kim's probably got other things on her mind than my love life.*

"So, how's it going with Dr. BeachBum?" Kim asked, the moment Dani swiped to accept the call.

"How did you know anything was going on?" Dani blurted, surprised by her friend's directness.

"Ah, so there *is* something. I didn't know. I only suspected. Spill it, bestie. What's going on between you and the sun-bleached beach boy?"

Dani couldn't suppress the smile that crept over her face.

"I knew it! There's more, isn't there? Tell me everything. What have you done, Dani? And don't forget—I know you better than anyone, so I'll know if you're holding back."

"Cade and I—"

"Oh, so it's *Cade* now, is it? Not Dr. Beach-Bum anymore. You two must be getting cozy."

"Yes and no. We've decided that while physically, things are going *very* well, neither of us is interested in a relationship right now. So we've agreed that it's just sex. No additional commitments."

She was surprised to see Kim make a face.

"Dani, are you sure that's going to work out for you?"

"Why shouldn't it? You used to do this kind of thing all the time during residency."

"Okay, first of all, ouch, but fair. You and I are very different people, though. I know you, Dani. You're a softhearted romantic. You like things that are heartfelt, you like tradition, you like feeling attached."

Dani shifted uncomfortably in her chair. Everything Kim said was true, but it wasn't the whole truth. She might like all of those things, but that wasn't what she needed from Cade right now.

"Maybe I'm trying to discover a different side of myself," she said.

"Are you sure that's what it is? Because I know Peter hurt you pretty badly."

"This isn't about Peter. And that was a long time ago." The entire reason things with Cade were going so well was because the situation was completely different from the way it had been with Peter. Without the emotional attachment, the expectations of a relationship and the royal obligations, she didn't have to worry about being devastated when things inevitably ended.

"Then what is it about?"

"It's about…having something that's just for me, just for right now. It's not for the public, and it has nothing to do with my royal obligations. As long as Cade and I keep things casual, and as long as no one else finds out, then everything we do can stay between the two of us. I've never been able to have a relationship before where it doesn't feel as though the entire state department is involved."

Kim paused. "I just don't want to see you get hurt."

"There's no chance of that. We've both been very clear about our ground rules."

"If you say so. Just…know that I'm here for you if you need anything, okay?"

Before Dani could reply, her emergency pager went off. Dani checked it and said, "Kim, I've got to go. There's a patient coming in on the helipad." She brushed the sand from her feet as she hung up, then jammed her socks and shoes back on before heading for the elevator to the roof of the medical center at a fast clip.

Dani was among the first to arrive on the helicopter landing pad. The unconscious patient was being unloaded onto a gurney, and a nurse had started bag ventilation. "Give me the vitals," Dani shouted above the thunder of the helicopter blades as they wheeled the patient toward the end of the landing pad.

"Twenty-seven-year-old female, recent surgery to repair a complex fracture to the right femur," the nurse shouted back. "Pulse rate and blood pressure low and falling, respiratory decreasing."

So everything bad, essentially. "You said recent surgery?" She said as they went on to the elevator.

"Patient was in a skiing accident last week and suffered a serious break to the right femur, requiring surgical intervention. Surgery was successful, but she's been slow to heal. Blood pressure has been variable."

"Any history of heart problems?"

"None known to us or to her previous hospital. She was meant to be transferred here because her family wanted a second opinion—the last hospital wanted to continue monitoring her low blood pressure, but her family wanted answers. She was stable during the trip here, but took a sharp decline just before the helicopter landed."

The nurse was keeping up the bag ventilation as she spoke. Dani couldn't see the patient's face very well, but she glimpsed a head of striking blond hair with a few purple streaks. Something about that hair sent off a faint alarm in Dani's distant memory, but she wasn't sure exactly what it reminded her of. She turned her attention back to the clipboard the nurse had handed her. The patient had recently suffered a complex broken leg. Either something had gone wrong with the patient's recovery, or some new problem had arisen. In either case, Dani felt out of her depth. With no immediately clear diagnosis, this was a case for a team, not for one doctor working alone.

She was relieved when the elevator doors opened on the cardiac wing and Cade stood there, ready to help. For once, she was more than ready to hand a case over to his expertise. They reviewed the case as they brought the patient to the OR and had her stabilized. They were joined by the head of the cardiology unit, Dr. Briscoe, as well as several interns.

As Dani ventilated the patient, her mind was racing. The patient might be stabilized, but this was a case with numerous questions. What could a broken leg have to do with a dangerously low heart rate? Undiagnosed bradycardia? This was a young patient, but perhaps that meant an undiagnosed congenital condition.

"We have a narrow window of time here," Cade announced to the team. "Opinions? Recommendations?"

"Could be an undiagnosed congenital condition," one of the interns suggested.

"Maybe," Cade replied. "What about the broken leg?"

The room was quiet. "Maybe that's just an extraneous factor," said another intern. "Or maybe the trauma to the leg created conditions for an undiagnosed heart condition to manifest."

"It's a valid theory," said Dr. Briscoe.

"No," said Dani. Everyone turned to hear. "The broken leg isn't extraneous. It's a key factor."

"What makes you so sure?" Dr. Briscoe asked.

"It's possible that trauma to the leg affected the patient's condition. But it's also possible that there's continued bleeding at the surgical site—that while repairing the leg, her previous surgical team nicked a femoral artery or vein, which would account for continued, unexplained bleeding."

Dr. Briscoe frowned. "Testing that theory would mean reopening the site for an exploratory surgery. If you're wrong, this could risk exposing the patient to unnecessary complications and a much longer recovery."

"It does put the patient at risk," Dani agreed. "But the risk of not reopening the site is greater."

"Agreed," said Cade. "I think Dani's reasoning is sound."

Dr. Briscoe gave Cade a long look. "It's your call," he said.

"Then let's see if Dr. Martin is right," Cade replied.

Eight hours of surgery later, Dani was back in the courtyard, exhausted. Cade sat next to her, breathing hard. There was no solitude this time—instead, every member of the surgical team had come along, sharing both the exhaustion and the enjoyment of a job well done.

Dani had been right. They'd reopened the site of the complex fracture to the patient's leg, only to find that somehow, the femoral artery had been completely severed. Dani surmised that the artery may have been nicked during the patient's first surgery, leading to a slow bleed, but over time, additional movement had put more stress on the artery, ultimately leading to a rupture during the patient's helicopter ride. She'd been in danger of bleeding out before the team had gotten her stabilized.

Dani was basking in the admiration of her colleagues.

"I'm extremely impressed you were able to form a diagnostic impression so quickly, Dr. Martin," Dr. Briscoe said. "I'm sure Miss Berlini and her family will be relieved to know that we've gotten to the bottom of her troubles with recovery and have been able to finally put her on the mend."

Dani's stomach dropped. "Did you say Berlini?"

"Yes—the family is quite prominent, I understand."

Those purple streaks in the hair. In the heat of working on the patient, Dani hadn't paid much attention to the patient's identity, and she'd been even harder to recognize because she'd been on a ventilator.

Dr. Briscoe was right about one thing. The Berlini family was indeed prominent. Angelica Berlini was the daughter of one of the wealthiest families in Europe, and she was also one of the biggest gossips Dani had ever met. They'd never exactly been friends, but they were more than acquaintances, having gone to the same school and most of the same social events over the years.

"Excuse me," she said. She needed to be sure. She went back to the patient's room. A nurse was recording vitals.

Now that Dani could get a good look at the patient, she confirmed that yes, certainly, this was Angelica Berlini. And the moment she woke up, she was bound to expose Dani's secret.

"How's she doing?" she asked the nurse.

"Extremely well," the nurse said with a smile. "Excellent work, Doctor. Everyone's very impressed. Now that she's on the road to recovery, she could be off the ventilator soon. Probably ready for discharge by the end of the week."

"Wonderful," Dani said, and she meant it. She was glad Angelica was going to be all right. But Angelica's arrival meant that the time for secrets between her and Cade was at an end.

She'd done her best to keep her promise to her family. But this was beyond her control. Angelica was Cade's patient as well as Dani's, and there was no way Cade wasn't going to talk to her as she recovered. And if Angelica saw Dani and Cade at the same time, she would recognize Dani instantly.

Even if there was some way she could contrive to speak to Angelica first and beg her to keep the secret from Cade, Dani found the idea distasteful. It was one thing for her to keep her royal status private. But asking someone else to actively help her cover up her identity felt too much like deception. Cade himself had said there was a difference between secrecy and privacy. Simply not mentioning her princess status to Cade felt like keeping her personal information private…even though it was a fairly important bit of personal information. But keeping that secret was the only thing that had allowed her to have a semblance of a normal life during her medical career.

But if she asked Angelica to outright lie about it… It didn't seem fair to Angelica or to Cade. And what if Angelica promised to keep silent, but then let something slip by accident? No. It was time to tell Cade. Sooner rather than later.

She braced her shoulder and left the room, determined to find Cade and explain that she needed to have a private conversation with him. But she immediately ran into Cade and Dr. Briscoe in the hallway.

"Ah! Here's our star fellow," Dr. Briscoe beamed. "Just the person I was looking for. Dr.

Martin, I'm so impressed with the diagnostic and surgical prowess you've just displayed that I want to reward you. I'm sending you away from Coral Bay."

She blinked in surprise.

"Just for a few days," he added quickly. "I'd like you to go to Horseshoe Cay at the end of the week on a recruitment mission. It's an island about half an hour away by seaplane. It's quite a bit larger than St. Camille, with three top-notch medical schools that are coming together to have a recruitment event. It'll be hospitals from all over the Caribbean giving presentations, trying to convince the brightest and best graduates to continue their training here instead of heading to the mainland."

"And you want me to go? I've only been here a few weeks."

"That's why I'd like it to be you especially. You're in the process of adjusting to island life right now. One of the biggest reasons doctors are hesitant to build their careers in the Caribbean is because of the adjustment to island life. Most of the doctors here at Coral Bay have been here for so long that those adjustments are only a distant memory—but they'll be fresh in your mind, of course. And the case we've just worked on would be an excellent one to present to new graduates. It's just the kind of exciting case that attracts top talent, and I'd like you and Dr. Logan to be able to talk about it firsthand."

By Cade's surprised expression, Dani could tell that this was news to him. "You want both of us to go?"

"It's up to the two of you, of course. This is a request, not an order. But it's something I hope will do both of you good. Dr. Logan, you've booked more time in the OR and cath lab than anyone else on the surgical team over the past few weeks."

"Well, I was needed," Cade murmured, but Dani noted the fine lines around Cade's eyes. Had he been overworking himself? She knew Cade well enough by now to know that he was the kind of person who would put in as many extra hours as needed, whether he was exhausted or not.

Dr. Briscoe huffed. "You're needed at your best, which means you need to slow down and let yourself take a break once in a while so you can be refreshed for your team and your patients. Now, there's a little room in the medical center's budget to spring for something a little more luxurious than usual. We're going to put both of you up in the Horseshoe Harbor Grand Hotel. Er, separate rooms, of course. The recruitment event is only for the weekend, but if the two of you would like to take a few extra days to relax, we can arrange for that. Let me know what you decide."

He headed back down the hall, leaving Dani and Cade together.

"Did Dr. Briscoe just send us on vacation together?" said Dani.

"I think so," Cade replied. "I've done a few of these recruitment events, and it's always a wonderful time. It's fun to explore the other islands, and Horseshoe Cay is quite beautiful. The hotel itself is something to see." He turned toward Dani, concerned. "But if it feels like too much, we don't have to do it. Or we can just go to the recruitment event and then leave, without staying for the extra days. You know, if spending that much time together feels too much like it's against the spirit of our arrangement."

Dani hesitated. She'd been worried he might be thinking the same thing.

"Of course, a little time off the island might be ideal," he continued. "We'd be away from anyone we know from St. Camille, so we wouldn't have to be as vigilant about keeping things private. It's a chance to have a little fun."

Fun. Wasn't that what Kim was always telling her she needed more of in her life? And what better chance to have fun than during a getaway with Cade, at what sounded like a fairly posh hotel?

"I can't wait," she said.

"Great. I'll tell Dr. Briscoe we're all in for the long weekend."

Dani was so excited by the idea of the weekend getaway that she didn't recall why she'd gone looking for Cade in the first place until after he left. She'd been prepared to tell him her secret until she'd gotten distracted by Dr. Briscoe.

Now, she realized there was a good chance that Angelica would be discharged from the medical center, and quite likely off St. Camille, by the time she and Cade returned. She didn't have to break her promise to her family. She didn't have to reveal anything.

Except...even after Angelica left, something like this could happen again. One of the reasons her family had allowed her to accept the fellowship was because Coral Bay had such a prestigious reputation among elite circles as a place for private recovery and excellent care. If Angelica Berlini could get medical care here, then so could any number of people who might know Dani's family. Her secret was safe, but only for now.

Once again, certainty hit her with blunt force. She had to tell Cade the truth.

But why? They'd agreed to keep things purely

physical. No romantic entanglements, no attachments, no obligations, they'd said.

So why did she feel obligated to tell Cade a
secret she'd promised her family she'd keep?

*Because you care about him. You care about
how he feels. You care if he feels that you lied
to him.*

Fine. Perhaps that was true. She cared about
Cade—as a person. But that didn't mean she
had feelings for him. She respected him. She
didn't want him to be hurt. And she knew Cade
would be hurt if he felt she'd lied to him. If she
actively tried to cover up her royal status, she
would be lying to him, no matter how she tried
to rationalize it.

She couldn't tell him yet, though. She thought
about what Dr. Briscoe had said about Cade
being overworked. Now that someone had mentioned it, Dani couldn't forget the tired lines
around Cade's eyes. She knew he needed some
time away. And that settled the issue in her
mind. She wasn't going to do anything that
would prevent Cade from having a relaxing
break, including revealing something that could
result in additional stress for both of them.

After they got back, though, she'd have to tell
him. And she'd have to find some way to explain to her family that telling very few trusted

people about her princess status was necessary, even unavoidable.

For a no-pressure, no-strings-attached situation, her affair with Cade was causing a surprising amount of stress. She knew she could find a way to deal with it. First, though, she was going to make sure Cade enjoyed their trip to Horseshoe Cay to the fullest.

Cade was glad to find that Dani was just as excited to leave St. Camille for a brief getaway as he was.

For one thing, he was excited to show Dani Horseshoe Cay. Even though St. Camille was, in his extremely biased opinion, the best island in the Caribbean, Horseshoe Cay had plenty to offer. The fine dining options were excellent, and he knew there would be a festival going on while they were there. And though their relationship was purely physical, he was excited at the idea of being able to spend more time with her. St. Camille was so small that the gossip flew at light speed, and any time he and Dani spent together outside his own home, they risked becoming fodder for rumors. On Horseshoe Cay, they'd be able to enjoy themselves away from any prying eyes.

In fact, he was already enjoying the benefits of taking their affair off-island. They were in the back of a small seaplane to make the short journey from St. Camille to Horseshoe Cay. Since they were the only two people on the plane, besides the pilot, he was able to hold her hand—something he hadn't been able to do in public for the past several weeks. He was glad that she gave his hand a returning squeeze. These short flights always made him nervous—it felt as though there was almost nothing between him and empty sky.

"I hate small planes, too," she said, noticing his apprehensive expression. "You can always feel the turbulence so much more."

Fortunately, it wasn't long before they were back on solid ground.

The medical center had very generously reserved two rooms for them. They were ornate, with four-poster beds and claw-foot bathtubs.

"It seems a shame that we're only using one of them," said Dani, sitting down on the king-size bed in his room.

"You're certainly welcome to stay in your own room," Cade replied. "I'm sure you're eager for some space after living in the medical center's dormitory for so many weeks."

"Space is nice," Dani said. "But this room comes with certain…amenities…that make up for having to share it."

"Oh?" he cocked an eyebrow at her. "What kind of amenities might those be?"

"Well. Take that bathtub over there. It's huge. Just think, if either of us had to use that bathtub alone, we'd practically get lost at sea."

"I see. So you're saying that it's much safer for *two* people to use that bathtub at once?"

"Only one way to find out," she replied.

Much later, after they'd spent quite a bit of time enjoying the bathtub, Cade suggested they go out and explore the town surrounding the harbor. Dusk had fallen by then, but Cade could hear music coming from the street.

"There's a fancy French restaurant about a block away from here," he said. "Or there's the festival going on this weekend—we've missed the parade, but the opening party will go on all night. There'll be street food and dancing. Which would you prefer?"

"Definitely the festival! Especially if there's food. I'm starving."

"Great. We can get stamp and go."

"Stamp and what?"

"You'll see. Let's go."

As they headed to the main part of town, the sound of calypso, drums and banjos filled the air. The town square was surrounded by food stalls and trucks, and in the center, people were dancing.

Stamp and go turned out to be a salty battered fish cake with sweet dipping sauce. Cade bought a large order from a food cart for them to share.

He smiled at seeing Dani licking her fingers with relish.

"This is wonderful," she said, her eyes closed with pleasure. "But why do they call it stamp and go?"

"It was the way British officers used to give orders on their ships," he said. "If they wanted something done in a hurry, they'd say 'stamp and go!'"

"That's not it," said the vendor of the food cart who'd overheard. "It's because it's so good that people used to stamp their feet while waiting in line for it."

Cade motioned toward the vendor. "Trust the expert," he said.

"Well, wherever it gets its name from, it's delicious."

They walked among the festival, admiring the various wares for sale. Dani kept turning an eye toward the dancing, and Cade had a feeling she'd want to join in as soon as they were done with their meal.

As they perused the various stalls, a man with a camera approached Dani.

"Excuse me," he said, "but I'm covering the

festival for a travel article in *The Sunday Times*. Do you mind if I take your picture?"

Cade was ready to jump at the chance, but to his surprise, Dani seemed hesitant—even startled. She went so far as to take a few steps back, positioning herself behind him. "No thank you," she said.

"Are you sure? I'd love to get a shot of—"

"She said no," Cade replied firmly. He put his arm around Dani and maneuvered her away from the stalls. "What was that all about?" he said, once they'd put some distance between themselves and the photographer.

"I just...really hate having my picture taken," she said.

"Really? Why?"

For the first time since he'd met her, she seemed at a loss for words. "I just do," she said. "I can't explain it. I'm just not comfortable with it."

"Enough said. If you don't like it, that's reason enough for me." Privately, though, he was a little confused. The request had seemed innocent enough, and it might have been fun to find their photo in the paper, or online, later. He knew that some people disliked seeing themselves in photographs, but he was surprised that a woman as gorgeous as Dani would feel self-conscious about how she appeared on camera.

The two of them had never taken a photo together. He hadn't given it much thought until this moment, but now that the subject had come up, he realized that he'd never seen her take a selfie, or suggest that they pose for a picture at any of the areas of natural beauty he'd shown her on St. Camille. Was she concerned that a photo could make others suspicious of their secret arrangement? Or was she simply camera-shy?

He wasn't able to ruminate on Dani's reluctance much longer, though, because a moment later, she pulled him into the dancing.

Cade had been to many festivals, but he hadn't been dancing in years. Dani was wearing a green dress with small white dots, and her skirt flared from her waist as she spun. She seemed to find the beat right away, falling into step with the dancers around her.

The last time he'd danced had been just before his wedding date. He'd taken classes to prepare for dancing at the reception, and then, of course, that hadn't happened. He'd given up dancing as part of his old life—and even if he hadn't, who on earth would he have danced with over the past several years?

His first instinct was to stay on the fringes of things. He was hesitant—uncertain of what to do with his hands and where to put his feet.

But then Dani grabbed his hand. She pulled him close, right there in the middle of the street. The other dancers whirled around them.

She pressed her hips against his and they swayed together. He could *feel* the drumbeats vibrating from the cobblestones of the street through the soles of his feet. But then he felt something else. It was the rhythm of him and Dani, a rhythm they'd perfected over the past few weeks, but one that promised there was still more to be discovered. He fell into that rhythm, trusted it, and suddenly, his body knew what to do.

He'd never danced with such confidence, but he was confident now. He followed the music and the natural motion of their bodies, and his heart thrilled when he heard Dani laugh with excitement.

Neither one of them wanted to stop moving. But for one moment, he did pause, bending his head toward hers. A hundred dancers surrounded them, twirling, clapping, laughing. But as his lips met hers, he felt as though they were the only two people in the world.

CHAPTER SEVEN

DANI FELT LIKE a different person when she and Cade returned to St. Camille. She was surprised to find that she even looked forward to returning to her cramped dormitory quarters. The medical center was beginning to feel like home to her.

During medical school, she'd enjoyed her time in Boston, but it was never more than a city she was passing through. She always knew she'd have to return home to Lorovia someday. She'd made friends, she'd grown as a physician, but she'd never really felt at home.

But St. Camille was different. She could see the palm trees swaying from the window of the plane, and she felt like they were waving hello. Her fellowship was only meant to be for three years, but she could see herself staying in a place like this forever. Making a life here.

But that was foolish. Thanks to her grandmother, her family was supporting her choice to work at Coral Bay, but would they continue to support her if she wanted to stay forever? Even if they did, what was here for her? As much as she was enjoying her time with Cade, her affair with him would only ever be an affair.

Even though she couldn't imagine how it would be possible, she did want more, someday. She'd always imagined herself having children. And as unlikely as it was, given her complicated situation, she'd dreamed of falling in love. But for right now, she was finding her situation with Cade to be enough. The fact that Cade *didn't* want those things took off a great deal of pressure. She could enjoy the moment.

Sometimes a little too much.

On their first day back at work, Dani had to acknowledge that both she and Cade were failing miserably at their attempts to avoid having physical contact with one another at work. If anything, their foray off-island only seemed to have inflamed their desire for one another. Dani had come to Cade's office to ask him a simple question about a recent surgery. The next thing she knew, she'd once again caught that cinnamon scent that wafted from his skin. A moment later, his hands were running through her hair, his body pressing close against her. His hands traced her side, caressing her breast— and there was no knowing how far things might have gone, had there not been a knock at his office door.

They broke apart, both startled. Cade smoothed his hair and Dani hastily checked her blouse buttons and straightened her clothes. They seated themselves on either side of Cade's desk, and Cade called, "Come in."

Dr. Davidson came in. "I'm glad to find you both here. I have an update on that case from the other week."

Dani tried not to panic. She and Cade had just returned from their trip. There hadn't been time to explain anything to him.

"I'm sure Miss Berlini's family was glad to have her home safe and sound," she said.

"Actually, she's still here."

Her stomach turned to ice. "What? I thought she'd be discharged by now."

"She was supposed to go home yesterday. But she insisted on staying an extra day. She wanted to thank you both for saving her life. I thought you'd want to have the pleasure of speaking with her. Her recovery's gone very well. You should both feel proud."

"We'll make sure to see her this afternoon," Cade said. "Just have the admin staff put it on our schedules."

"Yes, of course," said Dani faintly.

"Will do." Dr. Davidson gave another smile

as he left the room. Had it been a knowing smile, Dani wondered? Or was Dr. Davidson just being friendly?

It didn't matter. She had to tell Cade.

But before she could, he said, "You know what? I think you should go to meet the patient by yourself."

Her mouth was dry. "You...you don't want to talk with her?"

"I don't want to steal your thunder. The way you handled the case was outstanding, Dani. You should get all the credit. I'd only steal your glory."

He was handing her exactly what she wanted on a silver platter. She was in inner agony over what to do. Here was the chance to keep her secret and her promise to her family. On the other hand, he was bound to find out eventually—and wouldn't it be better if she told him sooner rather than later?

On the *other* other hand, telling him could change everything between them. And she wasn't ready for that.

"I don't know, Cade," she stalled, racked with indecision.

"Well, I do. Honestly, you'd be doing me a favor. I have an absolutely packed schedule thanks to that bit of time off we took. You'd really be helping me out."

She decided. If Cade didn't meet Angelica now, that would give her time to gather her courage and plan things out. She could tell him the right way.

"Well, if it'll help you out," she said.

"Thanks. I really appreciate it."

Dani sat at Angelica's bedside. "You're looking well, Ange. I'm so glad your surgery was a success."

"Me, too. The other doctors told me it was touch and go for a while. The worst skiing accident I've ever been in. I almost *died*," Angelica said with relish. Dani suppressed a small smile. Angelica was going to have quite a story to tell when she got home. She just needed to make sure Angelica was cautious about the parts of the story that she shared.

"I still can't decide what's crazier—my near-death experience or the fact that *you* were the person responsible for saving my life," Angelica continued.

"Ange, that's something I want to talk to you about," Dani said. "I've become a doctor. I work here at Coral Bay as a cardiology fellow."

"My goodness. A princess working as a doctor, of all things! How remarkably eccentric of you. But you always did have that unconventional streak."

"It is a little unusual for a member of my family to hold a job."

"Is something wrong? Has your family lost all their money?" Angelica's eyes were alight with the hope of fresh gossip.

"No, it's nothing like that. Being a doctor is just something I feel I'm meant to do."

Angelica's eyebrows furrowed. "I suppose everyone has their little quirks."

"But I need a favor from you, Ange."

"Anything. After all, you did save my life."

"My family is keeping my position here very quiet. We're not broadcasting it to anyone, or telling anyone outside the family about it. You're the *only one who knows*." Dani tried to put as much emphasis as she could on those last words, knowing they would appeal to Angelica's sense of the dramatic.

"A secret! How delicious. And I suppose you want me to keep it for you?"

"If you would. Please. It would just make things so much less complicated not to have to worry about photographers popping up unexpectedly."

"Well, I suppose I do owe you. All right, Dani. You don't need to worry about me. I won't tell anyone you're here."

"Thank you," said Dani, relieved.

Dani spent a few more minutes catching up

with Angelica, who enjoyed having Dani listen as she spoke of galas, red carpet premiers and parties. The more Dani listened, the more relieved she felt that she was in St. Camille, living the life she wanted, instead of being paraded around at events.

Later that day, when Angelica was finally ready to leave, she did so amidst much fanfare, giving tearful good-byes to the staff who'd taken care of her. At one point, just before leaving, she took Dani by the arm and said, "By the way, some of the doctors here are *extremely* handsome." She sent a meaningful glance in Cade's direction. "If all of them look like that, I can understand the appeal of working at a place like this." But as far as Dani knew, that was the only interaction Angelica had with Cade. So her secret was still safe. For now.

Over the next several days, Dani tried to find the right moment to tell Cade exactly who she was. But somehow, the right time never seemed to arise.

She couldn't help it. Not only had it been a long time since she'd had a relationship, it had been a long time since she'd had any *fun* in a relationship. It was nice for the two of them to be able to focus on each other. And Cade did seem incredibly focused on her. She could make no complaints about his attentiveness.

When they were apart, she wrestled with whether she was deceiving him. When they were together, all of her worries melted away. They were having so many delightful moments together, and it seemed a shame to spoil any of them with cold realities.

Cade had suggested he and Dani have a picnic on one of his favorite secluded beaches on the island. It was a little difficult to access because of rocky outcroppings, but the advantage of that was that hardly anyone ever used it, so they'd have the whole beach to themselves. Dani could see why this particular strip of beach was a well-kept secret: the sand was blindingly white, the water a perfect turquoise, and wind erosion had carved beautiful rock formations along the coast that kept the beach hidden from prying eyes.

They weren't quite alone, though. At the far end of the beach, a small boy was fishing.

"Looks like we'll have company for a bit," said Cade. "But no matter. The little fellow will probably head home once he's caught enough."

Cade spread a blanket for them. He'd brought along a picnic basket, which Dani was grateful for. They'd spent the morning enjoying the market in town, and she was hungry and tired after a long morning of shopping.

But before they could dig into their apples, cheese and white wine, a sharp cry echoed from down the beach.

Cade was off and running before Dani could even see what was happening, but she followed in the direction of the child's cry. As she drew closer, she saw what the trouble had been. The boy, who was probably no more than seven, had been fishing with a hook and a strong piece of wire. His line had become tangled, and in his frustration, he'd gotten it wound around his wrist. Now the wire was giving him some nasty cuts, though they didn't seem deep—Dani had a feeling the boy's cries were more from fear than actual pain.

Cade had his arm around him and was gently untangling the wire.

"Come now. Stay calm," he said, in a low voice. "We'll get everything sorted out in just a moment. Best thing you can do is stay still."

He unwound the wire and looked back to Dani. "Just a few cuts and scrapes here and there. He'll be up and running in no time." Indeed, the boy's tears had already dried, and he was looking at Cade with wide eyes.

Cade showed the boy how to coil his wire so it wouldn't tangle, which was no small feat for seven-year-old hands. Dani was struck by how patient Cade was, making sure the child could make the coil on his own and then demonstrating the best way to cast and recast the line into the water. Anyone who saw Cade like this, she thought, would be shocked to learn that he didn't want children. He had a natural instinct for talking to the boy at his level, and he waited patiently for the boy to master one step before moving on to the next.

Cade looked up at her. "This is Anton," he said. "He says it's his first time fishing, and his brothers told him he probably wouldn't catch anything."

"Well, then we'll just have to prove Anton's brothers wrong," said Dani. "I think he's been very brave, so far."

"I think so, too," said Cade. He gave the fishing line a practiced cast, then reeled it back in and handed it to Anton. "All right, kiddo. Try it again. Just like I showed you. It might take a few more tries, but I have a feeling that if you keep trying, you might be able to make your brothers eat their words. And your fish."

The little boy threw the line out, holding the coil just as Cade had shown him. Dani held her breath. She had never seen anyone fish before. The ocean was so vast that it was hard to imagine Anton's tiny hook catching anything.

But the boy's face was so hopeful, so determined. And then, all of a sudden— "A fish!" he screamed.

"All right, slow and steady, let's reel it in," said Cade.

Dani was absolutely enthralled, watching the boy reel in a small fish and put it into a nearby net with Cade's help. Little Anton caught two more fish before he trotted happily away from the beach, hauling his catch home.

"That ought to keep those brothers of his quiet," said Cade, his voice satisfied. They returned to their blanket and their picnic basket.

"You're great with kids," Dani said. "Can you really not ever imagine having any of your own?"

The smile dropped from his face. She'd obviously touched a sore spot, but she couldn't help feeling curious.

"I suppose I haven't told you why I became a cardiologist."

"We've never discussed it, no."

"It was because of my brother. Henry."

"I didn't know you had a brother."

"I used to. He passed away from an undiagnosed heart condition when he was only fifteen. I was eight at the time."

"Oh, Cade, I'm so sorry. I didn't know."

"Hardly anyone does. I've moved far away from the people who know this story."

"Can I ask how it happened?"

"Henry was a track-and-field star. But the running was too much for his heart, and his condition wasn't diagnosed until after he collapsed at a track meet. After he died, my parents started having problems. We all had different ways of dealing with it—my dad by leaving, my mom by checking out emotionally. And I dealt with it by going to medical school. I thought maybe I could make Henry's death mean something. Maybe I could prevent other kids from dying unexpectedly, the way he did."

"That's a lot of pressure to put on yourself."

"I can see that now. But at the time, it made a lot of sense to me. And I don't think I ever really let go of the idea—that it was my responsibility to fix everything. I believe some people may have experienced it as micromanagement." He smiled at her, and she smiled back.

"I think that's why I was in such a rush to get married right out of medical school," he continued. "I thought that if I couldn't fix my own family, at least I could create a family of my own. Start over. Start fresh. But then Susan left me for my best man—my best *friend*, a person who was essentially a brother to me. I'd cobbled together a family of choice out of friends and people I trusted. Losing those people made me realize that I couldn't handle loss, period. So I decided that relationships weren't for me." He shrugged. "You can't get hurt if you don't let anyone get close."

"What a hard thing to go through. I'm so sorry."

"Things have gotten better over the years. And I realized that I wasn't cut out for things like families or relationships. I decided that I didn't want children, because what if I passed on the heart defect that Henry had? Even if I didn't, children get into accidents, or they can catch illnesses. Anything could go wrong. The same with relationships. The more you get attached to someone, the more it hurts when you lose them. And I am never going to experience the loss of a loved one again if I can help it."

He meant it, she realized. And she couldn't blame him. After those kinds of experiences, who would want to get attached to other people? And why would Cade ever want to have a child, knowing the potential pain he could be facing if something went wrong? There were, of course, all of the positive sides to having a family, but she couldn't bring that up now, knowing the grief he'd experienced.

The strength of his belief that he would never want a family began to make her feel sad, and she knew why. Despite all of her intentions, she was beginning to feel attached to him. Even though they'd promised each other, over and over again, that that wouldn't happen.

She already knew the answer, but she asked him anyway. "Cade… Do you ever see your feelings on any of this changing someday?"

"I doubt it."

"Yes. So do I."

He looked taken aback. "But you're still okay with what we have, right?"

"Yes, of course." She gave him a faint smile.

"So there's no reason to change anything?"

"No," she said faintly. "I suppose there isn't."

Hours later, they loaded their picnic things into the back of Cade's car as the sun touched the horizon and created a golden path on the waves that stretched all the way to the beach.

It had been a perfect day, Cade thought. Somehow, his time with Dani always left him feeling more like himself. Like when they'd visited Horseshoe Cay and he'd felt so awkward when he first tried to dance. Something about Dani's presence let him relax and be himself. He'd felt it when he'd spoken about Henry earlier. He hadn't talked about his brother in years, and yet with Dani, it felt natural to do so.

Even though their relationship was just a

fling, she brought out a deeper, truer side of him. It wasn't like the fleeting relationships he'd had in the past. They had fun, but they talked about meaningful things, and he could tell he was better for it. He'd expected talking about Henry to feel painful, but instead it felt as though a weight of grief had been...not lifted, exactly, but eased.

He noticed that Dani had been very quiet for the rest of the afternoon. He hadn't thought much of it because up until now, the silence between them had felt peaceful, agreeable, but as it stretched on, he began to wonder if there was more to her silence than he first realized.

Suddenly he worried he might have put too much pressure on their relationship by telling her about Henry. This was just supposed to be a fling, after all. He'd brought up something emotionally heavy and, in doing so, had stepped out of bounds of their arrangement. She'd just confirmed that she didn't want to change anything about their agreement—that she was fine with what they had. But now he'd gone and brought up a very private piece of his own past, and he realized it could seem to Dani as though he'd made things too complicated, too personal.

"Is everything okay?" he asked as they folded the blanket together. "You seem a little distracted."

"Hmm? Oh, yes, everything's fine," she said, her gaze drifting away from him. Then she abruptly dropped her end of the blanket and turned to face the water.

He balled up the blanket and shoved it into the trunk. "What is it? Dani, if things got a little heavy for a moment, I'm sorry. I didn't mean to…"

She shook her head. Were those tears forming in the corners of her eyes? "No, it's not that at all. Please don't think that. I'm glad you told me about what happened to your brother, truly. It means a lot to me that you would share something so important with me. But Cade… it's made me realize that there's something I do have to share with you."

He reached out for her hand. "Hey. No, you don't. Everyone has a past. But this thing between us is about what's happening right now. Anything you might feel you have to tell me about the past isn't going to change how I feel about you today, or make me think differently about the person I know you are."

She met his gaze. Those *were* tears in her eyes, threatening to spill over. "That's the problem, Cade. I'm afraid that telling you this will change how you feel about me. I'm afraid it will change everything."

"Then why say anything?" He couldn't imagine what she could possibly disclose that would have an impact on how he felt about her. "We have fun together. Why should anything need to change?"

"Because despite our efforts to keep things uncomplicated, we're getting closer. I feel it, Cade. And I think you do, too."

Dammit. This was what came of unburdening himself, of sharing some of his most personal memories with someone. He had no one but himself to blame. By bringing up Henry, he'd opened the door to emotion, which they'd strictly agreed to keep out of their relationship.

And yet, he'd brought up Henry because he'd felt safe to do so. Some part of him had yearned to talk about his brother, and Dani, more than any other woman he'd met, made him feel safe when talking about his past.

Which meant that she was different from the women he'd known in the past. Which therefore meant that she was right: he was starting to care for her.

And from what she was saying, she was beginning to care for him, as well.

There were feelings between them now, no matter how hard he might try to insist there weren't.

"You're right." His words came out quietly, almost inaudible over the lapping of the waves.

"That's why I have to tell you this now. If I go on pretending, then both of us are going to get hurt."

"Pretending what?"

"To be a normal person."

His brows furrowed as he wondered where she was going.

"Cade, there's no easy or practical way to say this. I'm a princess."

He shook his head, at a total loss. "I don't know what you mean."

"I'm twelfth in line to the throne of Lorovia. My grandmother is the queen."

Lorovia? He'd heard of that country. His mind went back to high school geography classes. Lorovia was supposed to be a tiny country with a massive amount of wealth. Focusing on the details was helping him to control his rising disbelief that Dani could have kept such a large secret from him from the moment they'd met.

Perhaps that was unfair. In Boston, they hadn't known if they'd ever see each other again. But then she'd come to work at Coral Bay, and she hadn't told him. They'd been colleagues, and she hadn't told him. They'd become friends—they'd been intimate together—and she hadn't told him.

"Cade? Say something, please."

He was trying to, but his mind couldn't keep

up with events. Everything seemed to be changing around him, even though he and Dani were standing completely still.

He couldn't stop thinking about what this information about her might mean, let alone all the opportunities she'd had to reveal it to him. He'd thought he'd known who she was. This wasn't like revealing a mistake from the past, or having some sort of painful family secret. Dani had deliberately kept a fundamental fact about who she was from him.

"How could you lie me?" he blurted out. "Why didn't you say anything sooner?"

Dani looked extremely uncomfortable. "I never lied," she said, her voice miserable. "I just…didn't bring it up."

Her words were so similar to what Susan had said when he'd discovered she'd betrayed him with his best friend. Susan had never lied directly to his face, but she'd omitted so many truths that it amounted to the same thing.

Thinking about Susan brought back all the old pain—and the old anger—fresh, as though it had happened yesterday instead of years ago. "So everything that's happened between you and me—it was all, what, just some kind of prank? Or some way to amuse yourself?" His voice came out tight and brittle.

"No! Absolutely not." She was horrified.

"I had to keep it a secret for security reasons, Cade. It was never about keeping a secret from you, specifically. It's a secret I've had to keep for years from everyone but the most trusted people in my life. I know this must come as such a shock, but please try to understand. This was never supposed to hurt you. I never wanted to lie."

He wanted to believe her. Wanted to believe that she would never willingly hurt him. Moments ago, he'd been so certain that he knew exactly who Dani was, even though he was well aware that they both had much in their pasts that the other didn't know. He'd thought he didn't need to know any of the details. But that was when he'd thought he knew Dani.

"Cade, please don't stay quiet like this," she said, breaking into his thoughts. "I'll tell you anything you want to know. I'm not supposed to—my family won't like that I've broken protocol and told you about my royal status. But you're important to me. Please believe me when I say that I never wanted to hurt you, and that I'm telling you this now because I trust you."

She was saying that she trusted *him*? Right after revealing that she'd kept a huge secret from him? Doubt from the past kept setting off alarm bells in his mind.

"Is Dani Martin even your real name?"

She blushed. "No. My full title is Her Royal Highness Princess Danielle-Genevieve Matthieu DuMaria."

"Matthieu?"

"It's a family name."

He nodded slowly. "Okay. So your name isn't what I thought it was, you don't come from where I thought you did and you're not who I thought you were."

"I tried to explain, back in Boston, that my family situation was complicated. I couldn't tell you anything more then. I barely knew you, and my decision to practice medicine has always been a source of tension in my family. They've only allowed me to come here because the Coral Bay Medical Center helped my grandfather years ago. I'm not close in the line of succession, but I still have royal duties and a responsibility to uphold my family's image."

He thought of her refusal to be photographed on Horseshoe Cay. Had she been thinking about her family's image then? All he could think about was how it had been yet another opportunity for her to tell him the truth…and she hadn't.

The rational part of his brain could understand that there might be some logic to what Dani was saying. He knew that once he got used to the idea of her being royalty, he might be able to understand, on an intellectual level, that everything she was saying about needing to keep her secret very close made sense. But for right now, her words stirred the hurt of past betrayal. He couldn't shake off his shock at the news of her identity and that she had been capable of hiding it from him so well.

"Is…is there anything else you want to know about it?" she asked, her face streaked with tears. "I can explain more about the security measures or my family's expectations."

He shook his head. "The only thing I want to know is where it leaves us."

She took a deep breath. "It can leave us right where we are, if you want it to. With exactly what we agreed on. No emotional involvement, no attachment. It's the only kind of relationship I *can* have, Cade, because the obligations of a royal consort are so extensive that I can't casually date anyone otherwise. Trying to date when you're a princess is like… Imagine immediately having to decide whether you're going to marry someone on the first date and then asking for that kind of commitment."

As angry as he was, he tried to think about things from her perspective. "So there are a lot of rules regarding who you're with?"

"Not so much rules, as expectations. Anyone I was *officially* dating would have to sign an NDA, which tends to suck the romance and spontaneity right out of things. There are agreements to do public appearances and holiday events—and those are contractual obligations because otherwise the tabloids start making a fuss about every little thing in their search for a scandal, just because someone didn't make it to a holiday parade or a state dinner. And then there's the whole issue of living under a microscope—the press analyzing everything you do. So everything has to be kept secret, unless it's really serious."

"And we weren't serious." That had been the whole point, but he still felt a pang in his chest as he said it.

"We weren't supposed to be," she replied. "I thought the fact that this was just an affair would protect us. All of those expectations are a lot to put on someone. And the one time, years ago, that I was able to get someone to agree to all of them, it was a huge disaster. The only reason they agreed to put up with all of it was to get close to me, so they could make money by selling pictures to tabloids. I never know what's real, Cade. As a princess, I never know who's using me or who likes me for who I am. But with you I could just be myself."

His anger softened, just a little. Hadn't that

been what he liked about being with Dani? Around her, it was easy to be himself.

"Please believe me when I say that I was trying to spare you," she continued. "And since our relationship was *just* a fling, there was no need for you to have to sign anything official or participate in anything formal. But if the press got wind of it, or if I made any public appearances with you, we'd have to decide very quickly if we wanted to keep seeing each other. Otherwise, if the press thought we were in a relationship, but we had no formal agreement in place, the paparazzi could create a scandal out of thin air. I've seen it happen before."

"It sounds like you're saying that if someone else found out, we'd have to end things."

"We'd have to…make a choice. We could end our fling and let any rumors in the press die out. If there's no fire, there's no smoke. Or we could continue, but we'd have to present you to my family and formally commit to being in a relationship. Which is full of obligations I don't want to put on you." For the first time since she'd made her revelation, she looked at him with a glimmer of hope in her eyes. "Does this mean you…*don't* want to end things?"

What he wanted was a time machine that would let him go back to the point before Dani had revealed her princess status. But no, he realized, even that wouldn't fix things. He hadn't known the truth, and he couldn't be in a relationship with someone who wasn't truthful.

But she was being truthful now. She was telling him everything, even though it clearly cost her great effort to do so. Didn't that count for something?

She was waiting for his answer.

"No," he said, finally. "I don't want to end things. But maybe we should slow things down for now."

"I understand," she said, her voice tinged with sadness. "Take all the time you need."

The disappointment in her eyes pained him, but he couldn't bring himself to respond in any other way. He didn't want to end things with Dani. But he didn't want to relive the pain of Susan's betrayal, either. And no matter what Dani's intentions had been in keeping such a huge part of her life a secret from him—no matter how justified she might be—he was still in the position of hearing someone he cared about explain that they'd kept important information from him. Years later, the pain was still fresh, and he wasn't ready to face it.

But he wasn't ready to let go of Dani, either.

Something had to change, though. Dani's revelation that she was a princess was shocking enough, but the pain came from the fact that she'd been hiding such a huge part of herself from him for so long. The only way he could think for them to get through this was to take a few steps back. From what Dani was saying, it sounded as though a serious relationship between the two of them would be far more complicated than he'd ever realized, and he worked hard to avoid complications under ordinary circumstances. He needed time to wrap his head around everything and to know that he wouldn't risk getting hurt if further revelations came out. He hoped there wasn't more, but he needed to be prepared for the possibility.

"There's one more thing before we move forward," he said as they finished packing up his car. "Are there any other big secrets I should know about?"

"Just the one. I swear."

CHAPTER EIGHT

DANI TUGGED HER sweater tightly over her scrubs as she took the lab results from Nurse Johnston. "Thanks for getting these back to me so quickly," she said. "And do you have the results for the patient we talked about this morning?"

Nurse Johnston blinked at her. They both waited for a moment while Dani didn't respond. Then Nurse Johnston said, "You're holding them right now, Dr. Martin. I just handed them to you."

"Oh! Of course. I'm so sorry. My mind must have been elsewhere." Dani blushed furiously as Nurse Johnston walked away, shaking her head.

It wasn't like her to lose her focus like that at work. But ever since her beachside date with Cade, she'd had a hard time concentrating.

She knew that Cade's suggestion that they slow things down was completely reasonable. Still, she hated it. The past few weeks had been like a dream. She'd finally been able to connect with someone without any pressure or complications. She wasn't ready to give that up yet, even if continuing on together was a bad idea.

He didn't break things off, though. He just said to slow things down. Those were two different things.

So why did they feel the same?

They'd been unusually distant with each other over the past few days. There were no more clandestine kisses in their offices, no more meaningful glances after surgeries. Perhaps that was because work had become so busy. They'd barely had a chance to speak to one another at all.

Her phone buzzed in her pocket. It was the first text she'd received from Cade in several days.

Can you come over to my place as soon as you get off from work?

Finally. Maybe after a few days of caution, Cade was ready to relax a little.

Fifteen minutes later, her shift had ended. She headed away from the main atrium of the medical center to the staff dormitories. The halls were nearly empty, as usual. Most of the staff preferred to have their own homes on the island. Dani had an appointment with a realtor to find a place of her own later that week. She couldn't wait; she was looking forward to finally having her own space.

She showered, then began picking out clothes for the evening. As she dressed, she noticed that her phone had received repeated notifications while she was in the shower. Had Cade been trying to get in touch with her?

She picked up the phone and realized there wasn't one message waiting for her. There were hundreds.

She scrolled through them, and her heart sank. It was clear enough what this was all about.

Kim had sent her the worst of it. She'd forwarded Dani the pictures. They were blurry, but they clearly depicted her and Cade in the town square on Horseshoe Cay. The way they were dancing together made it clear that they were more than just friends—as did the kiss that had been caught on camera.

That photographer who'd wanted to take her picture had clearly gone ahead and done so, even without her permission. Dani wondered if he'd recognized her immediately or taken her picture and done his research later. Either way, the damage was done.

The headlines screamed with speculation. Who was this mystery lover of the princess of

Lorovia? How involved were they? Was the trip meant to be romantic? Perhaps a proposal was on the horizon and, with the proposal, a wedding and a family. One headline even speculated that she was already pregnant. Dani knew this was typical tabloid nonsense, but it still infuriated her. She might have gained a few pounds since her arrival, but that was merely the stress of adjusting to a new environment. But of course, no tabloid could resist a chance at body-shaming.

She kept getting more texts and alerts, even as she tried to decipher the messages that were already there. It seemed as though she had voice mails waiting from everyone she'd ever met, including her entire family, all of her friends and the Lorovian State Department. She'd have to take the weekend off from work just to return calls.

If there was one silver lining, it was that the tabloids barely showed interest in the fact that she was working as a doctor at Coral Bay. Her family's fear that her career would create a scandal was sorely misplaced. The articles briefly mentioned her profession, then went on to obsess over her love life and the utter fantasy that she was moments away from a proposal.

Had Cade seen the headlines?

What must he be thinking right now?

She scrolled back to Cade's message on her phone. There was nothing more after the message he'd sent earlier.

Can you come over to my place as soon as you get off from work?

And nothing else following her response.

Had he seen the photos before he sent the message?

If he had, the message took on a whole different context.

She'd been looking forward to a fun night of reconnecting, especially after they'd spent the last few days without much contact. But now her excitement evaporated into worry, tinged with panic.

What would he make of the headline insinuation that she was pregnant? She knew how much Cade didn't want children. If he thought she was pregnant, he must be frantic.

Calm down, she told herself. Cade was a practical man. Surely, he'd know that the headlines were nothing more than a grab for attention.

But it immediately became of the utmost importance that she talk to Cade. What if he didn't understand that the story was rumormongering, plain and simple? What if he thought the headlines were true?

She was used to the press interfering with her life. Her family had taught her from a young age that all of her choices would eventually become a matter of public discussion. But rumors that she was pregnant weren't merely hurtful to her. They also touched on a very private grief of Cade's. She knew how afraid he was of passing his brother's heart defect on to a child of his own. She hated to think that these headlines would cause him even a moment's pain.

This was exactly the reason she avoided relationships. It wasn't just about her own difficulty trusting again after Peter's betrayal. It was the fact that anyone she dated was also subjected to the same kind of scrutiny that she'd had to put up with for her entire life. It wasn't fair to someone else to have to go through that.

And now that Cade was getting a taste of exactly what she'd been trying to protect him from, she was certain he'd want to end things. The thought tore at her heart, even though she knew that ending things now was the wisest course of action. If they stopped, she could tell her family that the paparazzi was making something out of nothing, and the tabloids would eventually lose interest and move on to something else.

She left her dormitory and raced down the beach toward Cade's cottage. There was no choice for either of them. If they had to end it, they had to end it. But she hoped he would forgive her first.

Dani had tried to rehearse what she could possibly say to Cade as she raced down the beach. But any words she might have prepared abandoned her the moment he opened his door.

"I take it you've seen the photos," he said, the moment he saw her red, sweating face. She'd nearly run the whole way.

"Yes. Just now. My phone's blowing up with messages, but I wanted to talk to you before anyone else."

He waited while she caught her breath. When she could speak again, she said, "None of it's true, of course. It's all pure speculation. The more outlandish it is, the more papers they sell and the more clicks they get online. But it's just rumors, Cade. I swear. I never wanted you to get hurt like this."

He gave her a long look. "So you're not pregnant."

"Of course not! If I were, I'd have told you immediately. These are baseless rumors, and I feel horrible that you've been affected by them."

He let out a long, slow breath. "Affected by them? That's one way of putting it. When I couldn't get ahold of you, I didn't know what to think."

"I'm so sorry you were upset by this."

"Upset? I'm furious, Dani! You know how I feel about having children. And then, for the past half hour, I've had my face plastered all over the internet, with speculation that I'm about to become a father! People I haven't spoken to in years have been texting me congratulations!"

His eyes burned with rage but, more than that, with hurt. Dani felt miserable. She hated that Cade had been forced to deal with some of his worst memories, simply because he'd been photographed in a public place with her.

"This is all my fault," she said.

He let out a long, slow breath, and she could see that he was trying to control his anger. "It's not *all* your fault. You're not the one who took those photos. If I ever see that photographer again, I'll wring his neck."

"You can't do that, Cade. This is just a small taste of what life in the public eye is like. You can't use brute force against every single member of the paparazzi."

"I can try."

A dark laugh escaped her. "Not if you want to keep your medical license."

His mouth formed a thin, firm line. "If I had

known that you were a princess, I could have been more prepared. I would have kept my guard up on Horseshoe Cay, instead of thinking that we didn't have to worry about our secret getting found out since we were away from everyone we knew here on St. Camille."

So he did blame her, then. And he was right. That part was her fault.

"I should have told you sooner," she said.

"Yes! You really should have. Everything could have been different if you'd been honest with me."

"Cade, it was supposed to be a secret. I'm only allowed to tell people I trust completely."

"But why is it all about your trust? What about the fact that I'm affected by it? I could have made different choices—we *both* could have made different choices about how we conducted ourselves—if you'd shared your secret much sooner. Instead, you didn't tell me, and now this is happening. This is my life, Dani.

"When you told me you were a princess, at first I didn't believe you. Then I took some time to adjust to the idea. And I thought maybe we can make it work. Maybe there's a way to go on as we have been, not meaning too much to each other, but still having fun together."

It was bittersweet to hear he'd been spending the last few days wondering if they might have a chance. So much had changed since her confession on the beach.

"And now?"

"Now… I'm just trying to figure out how to deal with what's happening, minute by minute. My mother reads these kinds of tabloids. I'm going to have to explain to her that no, she's not expecting a grandchild. On top of the fact that she's also not about to gain a royal daughter-in-law."

Dani winced. Some of those headlines really had made it seem as though she and Cade were on the verge of getting married.

"I don't even know what everyone at work is going to think. For years, I've been able to keep my personal life personal. But now I've been getting calls, texts—about us dating, about fatherhood… Dani, it seemed like everyone else knew more about my life than I do. I felt completely exposed. I've spent most of my adult life trying not to feel that way."

"I know the feeling," she said. She remembered how she felt when the photos that Peter had sold were published. She'd felt as though someone had pulled back a protective curtain of privacy that she hadn't even known was there. "I never wanted to subject you to this."

"Dani, I…" He paused, and then seemed to push himself to go on. "Every relationship

I've had has been about avoiding getting close, avoiding loss. And then these photos came out. And they reminded me of all the reasons I've made those choices. All this speculation about me becoming a father to a child, about the two of us being on the verge of marriage... I can't do those things."

"I know that," she said. "We've always said from the beginning that that's not where things were going."

He hesitated, then added, "I can't do this anymore, either, Dani."

"I know," she whispered. Still, it hurt to hear him say it. Knowing that something was about to happen didn't change the way she felt about it.

She looked at Cade's blue eyes, looking back at her with concern. That was Cade. Even amid the hurt and anger he was feeling, he still found a way to have concern for her.

"I knew that everything would change once the press found out. I just thought we'd have more time."

"I'm sorry, Dani. I wish there were some way things could be different for us."

Wasn't there a way, though? She knew, even as she said it, that there was no hope, but she couldn't help herself from pointing out that there was one way forward for the two of them.

"I mean, we could always make things official," she said, trying to make her voice sound casual. "You sign on as my consort, fill out all the various palace legal agreements…"

"You can't be serious."

"Of course not," she said quickly. And she hadn't meant it. Not really. She and Cade had been very clear about their agreement from the beginning. She knew perfectly well that Cade wasn't interested in the kind of commitment that becoming a royal consort required. Who would be?

She couldn't possibly have expected Cade to say that none of it mattered—that he'd put up with anything, go through any amount of inconvenience and suffer any kind of public scrutiny—just to be with her. It was an unrealistic fantasy, and she knew it. Everything that had just happened was proof of just how unfair it would be for her to have those expectations of Cade, and why they'd agreed to no commitment in the first place.

But like most fantasies, it was hard to let go.

"Cade, I'm just curious. If I weren't a princess…and I really did want some of the things these headlines are suggesting, what would you want?"

He paused, and she knew that his hesitation told her everything she needed to know.

"Never mind," she said, quickly. "I shouldn't have asked. It was just a hypothetical question."

"I'm sorry," he said.

"You shouldn't be the one apologizing to me right now. I've just gotten your life turned upside down."

"I wasn't apologizing. I just meant that I'm sorry things have to be this way."

And that was the story of her life. No matter what she wanted, things had to be a certain way. She should be used to it by now. She shouldn't be feeling hurt or angry. She was the one who'd brought all the hurt into Cade's life. She was the one who'd kept a secret that had ended up causing all of this turmoil in the first place.

And so it wasn't fair for her to be angry or hurt…and yet, a small part of her was. Cade had every right to be upset. But he also clung to his belief that the way to deal with his feelings was to distance himself from everyone and everything that could cause him pain. She'd never really thought about how it would feel if one of those things he distanced himself from turned out to be her. After all, she'd never intended to get attached to him.

But in spite of all her best efforts, her feelings had changed. Cade's hadn't, and she had no right to expect them to.

"I should go," she said. She'd done what she

came to do and assured him she wasn't pregnant. He'd done what he felt he had to do and told her what she'd known all along: that they had no hope for a future together. How strange, she thought, that the things she already knew could still hurt her so much.

The silence stretched between them. Any wild hope she'd had that he might tell her not to go dissolved completely in that silence. She turned and left the cottage, and as she walked down the beach, she didn't allow herself to look back.

It had been a long time since Cade had been struck speechless. As Dani left, he longed to call out to her. He didn't know what he could possibly say, and it didn't matter anyway, because his words were stuck in his throat.

Living on St. Camille, he'd gotten used to one day being very much like the next. There were always different medical emergencies to deal with at work, but for the most part, his personal life was one of stability and routine. He liked it that way. There were no secrets, and thus no unexpected surprises.

But then Dani had come along. No one else had known they were together, and the agreement they had in place to keep their emotions out of their relationship had given him a sense of security. He'd never once felt out of control.

Until this afternoon, when he'd seen the pictures. The initial shock had been severe. If Dani had trusted him with the truth, he could have been prepared. Instead, he'd been blindsided. The headline speculating that she was pregnant had hit him particularly hard. The rumors had brought back all the reasons he was determined never to be involved with anyone again, especially anyone who wanted children.

In his heart of hearts, he did want children of his own. It was a wish he'd never shared with anyone, because he knew it would be impossible. The worry of passing on Henry's heart defect to a child of his own was always present. Atrial valve defects weren't always detectable via ultrasound, which was why procedures like the pulse oximetry screenings he and Dani had performed in the NICU at Coral Bay were so important. He didn't know how he could make it through nine months of a pregnancy, completely helpless to have any control over his child's well-being, with no way to know if his child was healthy until it was born.

By not having children—by avoiding relationships, and thereby avoiding marriage and any possibility of a family—he also avoided loss. But that meant there would be no small fingers to curl around his, like the newborns in the NICU. There would be no baby to cuddle, no child to teach and guide through their own small adventures each day. These were the sacrifices he had to make. The potential for grief was too great otherwise.

He should be relieved that none of the headlines were actually true. But his relief was overshadowed by his frustration with Dani. He couldn't stop thinking that so much could have been different if she'd told him the truth in the first place.

He might not have much experience with royalty, but he felt it was completely unfair that once they'd become involved with each other, she'd continued to keep her identity a secret from him. Before their involvement, he could understand the argument that she could only reveal her secret to the people she trusted most. But once they'd begun their fling, she should have told him, so that he'd known what he was signing on for. At least he could have been prepared. At least she would have acknowledged that it mattered to her exactly how much his life could be affected if their affair were to be discovered.

In some ways, this would be easier if he could regret that he'd ever gotten involved with Dani. But that would be another lie—this time to himself. Thinking about the heat and passion of their nights together, he knew he would have made the same decision, even if he'd known about her royal status. He just would have taken more precautions and been ready for the fallout when it came. And it wasn't only about their physical connection. He'd had fun with her and felt more like himself with her. Their connection had been real in a way it was never supposed to be. And that made him angry with himself, for letting his guard down, and with her, for not being the person he'd thought she was.

And that was the worst part. Because the person he'd *thought* Dani was, was absolutely wonderful. So wonderful that it terrified him.

He'd been so reluctant to admit it to himself, but the person he'd *thought* Dani was, was someone he could be close to. He'd been so concerned about his colleagues finding out about their affair and worrying—in part—about their judgement of him having an affair with a subordinate, even though workplace relationships weren't terribly uncommon on St. Camille. It was a small island, after all. But he knew now that if anyone had discovered their affair, he wouldn't have wanted to end it. It would have been worth any amount of scrutiny from his colleagues to be with the person he'd thought Dani was.

Now that it was over between them, he knew he'd have done anything to be with the person he'd thought Dani was. And that left him feeling off-balance, because he didn't do commitments or relationships. He'd done without relationships for a long time, and this should be proof that he didn't need them.

It was frustrating, then, that he still yearned for her. He missed her conversation, her humor and the feeling of her body next to his. He ached for her in spite of himself, in spite of knowing that the person he longed for had fundamentally hurt him. He wanted her back, and he also never wanted to see her again, because the degree to which he wanted her back alarmed him. He'd been a fool to ever think they could just have a fling. It was for the best that they'd ended things when they did, because if they'd stayed together much longer, his heart would have been in serious danger of becoming entangled.

He didn't think her suggestion that he become her official consort was as casual as she'd tried to make it sound. But he couldn't give it serious consideration. The obligations sounded extensive, and he had a career on St. Camille. If his relationship with Dani became official, would her family understand how important his career was? Or would they expect him to play some over-puffed role in the public relations wing of the royal family? They'd been reluctant to allow Dani to have a career as a doctor; would they understand how important his profession was to him? He couldn't imagine giving up his life in the Caribbean to spend his days attending state functions for a country he'd never even visited. Maybe Dani had been joking, after all. In fact, he recalled, she had been the one to first suggest they keep their fling a secret. From the start, she'd never envisioned a public relationship with him.

A serious relationship between the two of them would never have been possible. He knew that now. But his heart was having a much harder time accepting that reality than he could have ever predicted.

Even if Dani wasn't royal, he could never give her everything she wanted. He knew she wanted children, but the thought of loving and potentially losing a family again was simply too much to bear.

There were a thousand reasons why ending their relationship was the right thing to do. He knew it, and he knew she knew it, too. He just wished it didn't have to hurt so much.

Dani stormed along the beach, furious with herself.

She couldn't believe she was in this situation

once again. Cade was different from Peter, but the end result was still the same. She'd gotten close to someone, and the press had made an appearance just in time to ruin everything.

Maybe it was for the best. Cade was never going to want a deeper relationship with her. And it wasn't fair of her to hope for that, when he'd been clear about his intentions from the beginning. It wasn't as though he'd led her on. She'd agreed with Kim that Cade wasn't right for her. The whole *point* was that Cade wasn't right for her. He didn't want a relationship or a family, and that wouldn't change.

She looked at the tabloid photos on her phone again. She knew she shouldn't, but it was so hard to tear herself away. At least she could get a small laugh at the headline speculating that she was pregnant. Imagine. So she was a little heavier than usual. The press didn't need to leap to ridiculous conclusions about it. Why, she'd just had a period three weeks ago.

The thought stopped her midstep. It had been three weeks ago, hadn't it? Or perhaps four. She'd been so busy that she'd lost track of a few things.

It had to be three weeks ago. It had been the strangest period, though. Just three days of light spotting, and then nothing.

This was ridiculous, she thought. There was

no way she was pregnant. There would have been other signs. And she was a doctor, for heaven's sake. She knew her own body.

She hadn't had any nausea, except for a few times in the morning after she'd had some bad soup for dinner from the medical center's commissary. Once she'd realized the connection, she'd stopped eating the soup. But she'd still been queasy for a few days afterward.

She began walking down the beach again, but more slowly. She was going over details in her head. Her late cycle could be attributed to fatigue. She'd been very busy, after all. Her body was a little more swollen than usual, but again, she'd been very busy, with no time to exercise. And she couldn't prepare her own meals while she was living in the dormitory. Which also could explain the nausea she was experiencing, as she couldn't always choose the healthiest meal options when she was busy. There were perfectly plausible explanations for everything she was experiencing. In fact, pregnancy was probably the *least* likely explanation for her symptoms, because she'd been on contraception ever since she and Cade had started their fling.

That stopped her thoughts for a moment. She'd started taking the pill *after* that first night with Cade. And while they'd used protection every night since, on their first night together, they'd used a condom from her purse. Her "wishful thinking" condom—the one Kim had put there years ago.

Most condoms began to break down after a few years. Dani couldn't remember exactly how long that particular condom had been sitting at the bottom of her purse. Had it been two years? Three? Or perhaps even longer than that? She hadn't had any reason to give it much thought. The condom was never supposed to be anything more than a bad joke, but now, nothing could be more serious.

Her worry grew stronger by the moment. They'd used an unreliable condom. And she'd made the biggest mistake a doctor could make: she was trying so hard to explain away her symptoms that she hadn't considered all the possibilities. Especially the possibility that she might actually be pregnant.

She needed to take a pregnancy test. Immediately. Once she had confirmation that she wasn't pregnant, she could put the questions that swirled in her mind to rest. And if she was pregnant… Well, she'd cross that bridge if she came to it.

She changed direction and walked toward town as quickly as she could.

CHAPTER NINE

BEFORE SHE'D EVER arrived on St. Camille, Dani had wondered if it might be difficult to adjust to life on such a small island. Now, for what felt like the thousandth time, she felt awash with gratitude for how close together everything was on the island.

The closest drugstore was only a ten minute walk from the beach. She'd briefly considered going to a different drugstore that was farther away from Coral Bay. That way, she'd be more sure of avoiding running into anyone from work. But the thought of spending an additional minute with the uncertainty that swirled through her mind was unbearable. She couldn't wait. She needed to put her fears to rest as soon as possible, and that meant buying a pregnancy test right away.

She grabbed a test off the shelf, then hastened to the checkout aisle—only to run right into

Nurse Johnston, who had apparently gotten off her shift recently as well.

Nurse Johnston gave her a warm smile. "*Bonswa*, Dr. Martin," Her eyes drifted to the package in Dani's hands.

"*Bonswa*, Nurse Johnston. Just picking up a few things." Dani hastily tossed a few random items from a nearby shelf into her arms, but the damage was done. She knew Nurse Johnston had seen exactly what she was holding and had probably seen the tabloid headlines, too.

Her worries were confirmed a second later. "The papers are saying you're a princess, Dr. Martin. But I hope you know that all of us at Coral Bay consider you a friend, first and foremost."

Dani blushed, feeling grateful. "That's very kind of you, Nurse Johnston. I feel the same way."

"I just wanted to mention it in case you could use a friend to talk to about now." She gave a meaningful look at the items in Dani's arms.

Dani adjusted the items to give more cover to the pregnancy test, for all the good it would do now. Both of them knew perfectly well that Nurse Johnston had seen what she was holding. But any explanation she tried to give would only make things worse. All she could do was stammer, "Thanks. I... I'll keep that in mind."

She paid for her items, double-bagging them in the hope that her purchase would be hidden from any other prying eyes she encountered on the way home. She couldn't imagine what Nurse Johnston would do with the news that she'd spotted Dani buying a pregnancy test. Everyone on St. Camille was kind, but gossip spread quickly. Cade had been right when he'd told her that there were few secrets on an island this small.

Back in the privacy of her dormitory, she took the test and awaited the results.

It was shocking how quickly the tests worked nowadays, she thought. One moment, she'd been taking the test and telling herself she was only doing it as a formality to calm her ridiculous fears. And then, two minutes later, her life had completely changed. The test was positive. She was pregnant.

She sat on her bed with her hands on her knees, letting her mind and body absorb this new knowledge. She'd been denying the possibility of pregnancy so fiercely. And yet, shouldn't all that denial have been enough to clue her in to the fact that something had changed? At the very least, she shouldn't be feeling so surprised.

If she was surprised, she couldn't imagine how Cade was going to feel. Especially after she'd spent the afternoon reassuring him that she wasn't pregnant. Insisting that the whole thing was an exaggerated tabloid rumor, designed to create a scandal. She knew he would be alarmed, and not just because she'd have to go back and tell him that she'd made a mistake, and that everything she'd said earlier wasn't true. She knew that he was afraid for the health of their child, and that he would rather close himself off from relationships than go through grief again.

The strange thing was that she wasn't filled with dread. Less than five minutes ago—before she'd taken the test—she would have been horrified to think of what she would have to tell Cade.

But now, she felt a clarity that she'd never had before in her life.

Her royal duties and responsibilities had often impacted, or even prevented, her pursuit of certain dreams. She'd tried to cope with that by accepting certain limitations. For example, she could be a doctor, but only within the time limit her family allowed. She could be with Cade, but only under the condition that they not become emotionally attached. These weren't just limits that others placed on her. They were limits she agreed to out of a sense of responsibility.

But now that she was pregnant, she realized she'd never wanted anything more than a family.

She knew that learning about the baby would be difficult for Cade and difficult for her family. It wasn't typical for members of the royal family to be single mothers, but it wasn't unheard of, either. This had happened before. But no matter how Cade—or her family—reacted, her path was clear: she was going to make certain that her child received all the love and support it deserved, no matter how anyone else felt about it.

If Cade didn't want to be involved, she'd make things work on her own. As far as her family was concerned, she'd have to see how they responded. She was sure that once they got over their initial surprise, they would rally around her with support. Her family might place heavy emphasis on tradition, and she had a feeling that some of her uncles would probably be more preoccupied with how to manage the narrative of her pregnancy in the press than with her actual child, but she trusted that they would also be there for her when she needed them.

And she would need them. Princess or not, she didn't think single motherhood would be easy. Despite the clarity she'd felt a moment ago, questions swirled through her mind. How would raising a child affect her career? Her family might want her to raise her child in Lorovia, but what if she wanted to keep working at Coral Bay? How would Cade feel about that? If he didn't want children, then how involved would he want to be? He would probably do the noble thing and help raise his child—but would he do that because it was what he wanted, or because he felt obligated to do so? How would she feel about having Cade in her life just because he felt obligated to be? How would a child feel about that?

There were more immediate problems to worry about as well. The press was sure to explode once her pregnancy was confirmed. She felt a twinge in her heart, knowing that this would affect Cade. There would be no way to hide that he was the father. Whatever reaction he had to the news, it would be public. She could try to ask for some favors from the palace public relations department, but there was probably very little she could do to protect his privacy.

She took a deep breath and told herself to worry about one problem at a time. First, she needed to tell Cade. There'd been enough secrets between them, and she wanted to share this one as quickly as she could. The other questions, such as where she would live and what would happen with her career—those could all be addressed later on. None of it would be easy, but she would make it work. With or without anyone's help.

The next morning, Cade walked into Coral Bay early. He'd had a sleepless night, wondering what it would be like to see Dani at work. They were both professionals, and he knew they would be able to find a way to work effectively together, but he still wasn't looking forward to the awkwardness of trying to be nothing more than colleagues again.

It didn't help that everyone else on staff seemed to be giving him sidelong looks of disapproval. He might have imagined it, but he could have sworn that Nurse Chapel had frowned at him when she'd handed him a file. Dr. Davidson had the look of a man with a suspicion confirmed. Everyone, apparently, had seen the photos and drawn their own conclusions about him and Dani from them. The disapproval he felt in his direction only made him feel worse, as it only served to highlight that he and Dani were no longer together.

He'd never been in this situation before. Should he call a staff meeting? Send a hospital-wide e-mail? Both of those ideas were probably terrible and likely to make things worse. Besides, the rumors weren't just about him.

They were about Dani, too, and he didn't want to take any action to address them without consulting her.

Gossip thrives on gossip, he told himself. If he ignored the gossip for long enough, it would die down on its own.

He was waiting in line for coffee at the commissary, when he overheard a group of nurses having a hushed conversation just ahead of him.

"Are you sure it was a pregnancy test, Marie?"

"Of course. I saw her buy it last night with my own eyes."

"Maybe it was for a patient."

"Then why wouldn't she requisition it from the medical center? I'm telling you, Dr. Martin was buying that pregnancy test for herself, because of all those rumors about her and Dr. Logan in the tabloids."

"Those two have been carrying on for a while. It's the worst-kept secret on the island. I didn't know she was royalty, though."

Cade's blood froze. The line moved ahead without him. He ducked out of the commissary and headed back to his office, his mind racing.

Dani had assured him she wasn't pregnant. She'd insisted that the tabloid headlines were just malicious gossip.

But if that were true, then why had Nurse

Johnston been whispering that she'd seen Dani buying a pregnancy test last night?

He didn't want to believe it. She'd looked him right in the eye and told him the tabloids were simply stirring up baseless rumors to get attention. Surely, she hadn't made all that up just because she thought it would make him feel better. Had she?

Another implication hit him like a punch to the gut. If Dani was lying, that meant she was pregnant.

For a moment, wild fantasies came rushing in. That dream of small fingers wrapped around his. A child with Dani's hair and his eyes.

But the images in his mind dissolved as all the old fear came rushing back. He couldn't have a child. More importantly, he couldn't stand the thought of losing a child. He couldn't lose another loved one. Not again.

Perhaps, he thought, Dani hadn't outright lied. Maybe she'd only bought the pregnancy test because she wasn't as certain about her situation as she claimed to be.

But if that were the case, why wouldn't she have told him?

Then again, Dani hadn't exactly been forthcoming with him for most of the time he'd known her. If she could keep a secret about being a princess, then why not keep this secret as well?

But she wouldn't keep a secret this big from him. At least, he didn't want to think she would.

He turned a corner into the next hallway and, suddenly, there she was. They stopped just short of running into one another.

"Cade, we really need to talk," she said.

His unease skyrocketed. "About what?"

"Can we go somewhere private?"

He was about to respond when his pager went off. "I'm needed in the cath lab."

Dani's pager buzzed as well. "Apparently, so am I."

They walked quickly down the hall in uncharacteristic silence. There was so much Cade wanted to ask her, but he had a feeling that not a single one of his questions could be answered in just a few minutes before a cath lab procedure.

As he and Dani stood side by side, scrubbing in before entering the cath lab, he couldn't hold it in anymore. It was a simple yes or no question.

Dani, are you pregnant?"

Her stricken face gave him the answer. "How did you know?"

There was no time to respond. They'd just finished scrubbing in and couldn't delay entering the lab. And it was lucky they didn't, because they walked in to a patient in active cardiac arrest, with one nurse giving CPR and another connecting defibrillation pads.

"Why weren't those preconnected?" Cade barked.

"Never mind that. Give us the history," Dani said.

"Forty-year-old woman who came into the ER last week with chest pain. She was scheduled this morning for a stress test, echocardiogram and MRI," one of the nurses responded. "We were doing a cath insertion when she went into arrest."

Cade raised his eyebrows, and noted Dani was surprised as well. Forty was young to need so much cardiac testing, let alone for a heart attack.

Dani took over the defibrillator paddles. After a few tense moments, the patient's heart was beating, though she still showed signs of tachycardia. Cade pushed calcium channel blockers to regulate the heart rate.

Within a few moments, the patient's eyes were open, and she was breathing on her own. "Don't try to sit up," Dani told her. "You've had a heart attack. You're going to be feeling very weak for a while, but Dr. Logan is going to get to the bottom of things and find out why your heart is acting this way."

As absorbed as he was with the patient, something about what Dani said caught at Cade's mind. Usually Dani told patients "*We'd* get to the bottom of things," referring to the entire care team. But just now, she'd referred specifically to him. Why was she leaving herself out?

He couldn't think about that now. He needed to focus on his patient, who had come in for a transradial cardiac catheterization.

"Do I still have to have the procedure today?" the patient asked.

"I'm afraid it's more important than ever, now that you've had a heart attack," he replied. "We'll insert a catheter through your wrist and then through a blood vessel into your heart, which will make the arteries show up very clearly on X-rays. Then we'll be able to see what's going on." He tried to infuse as much calm into his voice as he could, but inside, his nerves were frayed.

Once the patient was under local anesthetic, he began with a small incision into her wrist. Dani came and stood beside him.

"Are you planning on going somewhere?" he muttered.

"We'll discuss it later."

What was that supposed to mean? If she was pregnant with his child, then he needed to know where she was going and for how long.

Somehow, he made it through the hour-long procedure. The patient turned out to have a 99 percent blockage in the main descending artery, which meant that without proper diagnosis and treatment, a fatal heart attack could happen at any time. Cade was able to schedule the patient to have a stent placed at the site of the blockage, which would restore blood flow—and not a moment too soon.

"It's funny," he said, as he and Dani wrapped up the procedure and removed their surgical gloves. "The chest pain that woman had last week probably saved her life. She seemed to be in good physical health. If she'd ignored her chest pain, she might have had her heart attack anywhere other than a cardiac cath lab. And we wouldn't have discovered her blockage."

"She was so young to have heart problems," Dani replied. "I suppose it just goes to show that none of us can predict what's around the corner."

He'd been able to get absorbed in the successful treatment of his patient, but the relevance of her words brought him crashing down. "Like, for example, an unexpected pregnancy?"

She blushed. "Just like that. Yes."

"Were you going to tell me?"

"Of course! I was on my way to tell you. But then we had a patient. How could you think I wouldn't tell you? And did you know in the first place?"

"There's a rumor among the nurses that you bought a pregnancy test."

"Nurse Johnston," she muttered. "I was hoping she wouldn't spread that around so quickly."

"I thought we were done with secrets."

"Cade, I was going to tell you. I just didn't have time. Apparently, I had a secret from myself. When I first talked to you yesterday, I didn't think I needed a pregnancy test. I was so sure I wasn't pregnant. We'd been so careful. But then I realized, that first time, we used an older condom from my purse. I didn't think about how old it was at the time. I was just sort of…caught up in the moment. I'm sorry. At the time, I didn't think this could happen."

As angry as he was, seeing Dani so sad cut him to the core. He could be angry with her for keeping secrets, for lying to him about her royal status and possibly lying to him about her pregnancy, but it took two to make a baby, and even in the midst of his anger, he knew that the fact that she was pregnant was not her fault. "Neither of us were thinking about what could happen," he said, remembering the heat of that first night, the way they'd pursued each other with such reckless abandon. Recklessness. That had been the most exciting part of it. And now they were dealing with the fallout. "We had…other things on our minds."

It would be nice to believe Dani hadn't lied to him intentionally. Because now that he no longer had a patient to focus on and the confirmation of Dani's pregnancy was sinking in, a hundred conflicting emotions were hitting him in the gut all at once.

"What do you need from me?" he said. He felt completely overwhelmed by the news, but now that it was confirmed to be true, the only thing he knew for sure was that he had to support Dani and the baby. He'd decided to never have children, but if one was going to arrive, he had every intention of being the father his child needed.

She gave him a confused look. "Need from you?"

"Yes. I know you're royalty, but if there's any way I can support you or support the baby— any way at all—just let me know." He thought he was being remarkably chivalrous.

"Hmm," she said. "Here's something I need from you, Cade. I need to know how you feel about having this baby."

His head spun. He tried to buy himself time. "I haven't had much opportunity to absorb the news yet."

"Neither have I."

Fair enough.

But his brain was still fighting to catch up to the situation. Any relief he felt at the idea that she hadn't lied to him intentionally was overshadowed by the fact that she was pregnant with his child. He'd spent years avoiding the very possibility of that happening with anyone.

The thought of being betrayed again by someone he loved was bad enough to keep him from seeking out a relationship. But the thought of losing another family member, especially a child of his own, was unbearable.

But he couldn't tell Dani that. She was pregnant; she should be focusing on their child, not on his grief. If a child was coming, he'd simply have to find a way to bear it. He wasn't one to shirk his responsibilities.

"I need to know, Cade. How do you feel about this baby?"

He took a deep breath and mustered all his strength. "My feelings are that…if you're pregnant, then I'm here for you. I want to be here for you. For whatever you need. Whatever our child needs. Even if there's nothing between the two of us, I want to be in the baby's life. It's my responsibility, and it's the right thing to do."

"I thought you'd say something like that. I know doing the right thing is important to you, Cade. I know perfectly well what a noble person you are. But what about what you *want*? How do you feel? Are you excited about the baby? Afraid?"

He tried to respond, but couldn't get the words out. A week ago, it would have been the most natural thing in the world to tell Dani exactly how he felt, even about something as shocking as this. But that had been back when he thought she was someone else.

"You can't tell me, can you?" she said, her voice tinged with sadness. "You don't trust me anymore."

"I don't," he said. "But that doesn't mean I wouldn't take responsibility for my own child."

"There's that word again. I grew up in a family where everyone cared about things like duty and responsibility. And those were important things. But I've learned, Cade—I've learned in part thanks to you—that those things aren't everything. Love isn't a responsibility or a chore. It isn't about doing what other people expect you to do. I know what it feels like to live a life based on meeting obligations. And I don't want our child feeling that the only reason its father is in its life is out of a sense of duty, rather than out of joy. Can you honestly tell me that you actually want to be in this child's life? Even though you've always said you don't want children?"

He hesitated. "What I want doesn't matter.

The baby's coming, and I'm not going to abandon either of you."

She gave him a smile filled with tears. "Cade, I think I want something from you that you're not able to give. You and I, we decided from the start not to get emotionally involved. We wanted to have fun and to help each other break a long dry spell. And I know now that I wanted the fantasy of a normal life—a relationship without complications. I wanted that with you. But you know as well as I do that that kind of fantasy breaks down the moment a child comes into the picture."

"Don't you trust me? Don't you think I would do anything to protect a child of my own?"

She thought for a moment. "I believe you'd do anything you were capable of. So I'm going to ask you now—are you capable of telling me, in all honesty, that you want a child?"

He didn't know how to make her understand. The truth was, he *did* want a child. He wanted the tiny fingers wrapped around his, and the little body he could lift up to his shoulders to see the world.

But he didn't want the frightening part of it. He dreaded the nine months of pregnancy, during which he wouldn't know if his child had inherited Henry's heart defect. And even if Dani gave birth to a healthy infant, free from Henry's defect, there were plenty of other things that could go wrong. The patients he saw coming into the pediatric unit every day were proof of that. Becoming a parent meant shouldering the burden of constant worry that some harm could befall his child. The world held so many dangers that were out of his control.

That was what made him hesitate. And in that moment of hesitation, Dani said, "I didn't think so."

If it weren't for the fear, he would have promised her anything. Every impulse within him was telling him to beg her to stay. The idea of staying with her, and raising their child together, had woken a dream he'd left buried for years.

The more he thought about the reality of having a child with Dani, the more his anger and resentment toward her fell away. The truth was, he wanted all the things she thought he didn't want. He wanted a family, and what was more, he wanted her, complications and all.

But he couldn't face the risk of loss. All of the complications he and Dani faced made loss even more likely. What if she'd never wanted more than a fling with him, but was acting out of her own sense of obligation because they were about to have a child? What if they tried a long-term relationship and her family felt he wasn't good enough for her, or he didn't match up to their standards? And, of course, what if he lost his child, or Dani, to illness or injury? A thousand things could go wrong. His fear won out. He couldn't tell her that he wanted her because he could lose her.

Instead, he tried to explain. "You know why I've never wanted children. You don't know what it's like to lose a family member. You asked me to be honest with you, so I will be. No, I don't want a child. I don't ever want to go through that kind of loss again."

"So you're going to solve that problem by never getting close to anyone in the first place?"

"It's complicated," he said.

"I used to think that," she replied. "Funny how uncomplicated things get the moment you're pregnant."

"Dani...you know what could happen. You know that both of us could be facing significant grief."

"I know that even with a close relative, the odds of a baby having a heart defect are statistically low. And I'm not going to rob myself of any joy now, just because of something that may or may not happen in the future."

He couldn't agree. As a doctor, he knew of far too many negative possibilities to think about the positive ones.

After a moment, she said, "I need to go home to Lorovia for a while."

"For how long?"

"I'm not sure. There are…so many things to figure out. I'll have to explain to my family about the pregnancy. They'll all have their different opinions about how to handle it publicly. And someone from the palace will be appointed to stay in contact with you."

He hated to think about her working through all of those issues alone. He longed to tell her that he would be there for her. But saying that would mean making a commitment that he wasn't ready to give.

Also, what did she mean by "someone from the palace"? Would they honestly need a liaison to communicate? "You're making it sound as though it might be a long time before we see each other again."

She avoided his gaze. "The chief of staff said I could take as long as I needed. He said it might be a good time for me to be off the island for a while, since my secret identity's been revealed. That will give all the rumors a chance to die down a little. Then, if I ever decide to come back, people will have had time to get used to the whole princess idea."

"*If* you ever come back?" Of all the shocks

he'd had over the past few days, this one was the worst.

"Don't worry, Cade. No matter what happens, I'd never prevent you from seeing our child whenever you wish."

While that was reassuring, the thought of Dani not being in his life filled him with despair.

This, he realized, was everything he'd tried to avoid for the past several years. He'd done everything he could to avoid loss, but now he was losing Dani, and it felt as though his heart was being torn out. Even if she did plan to come back, things would never be the same between them. He might see her, she might stay in his life as the mother of his child, but he wouldn't have her. Not the way he used to.

Losing someone he cared about felt even worse than he remembered. He hadn't realized how much life she'd breathed into his days. Being around her had made him feel fresh and alive in a way he hadn't felt before, possibly ever, in his life. And losing her was everything he'd feared.

But he couldn't bring himself to tell her to stay or to take him with her to Lorovia. If losing her hurt now, it would only hurt more if they tried a long-term relationship and it didn't work out. Especially with a child involved. And there were so many reasons it might not work out.

"I don't know what I'm going to do next. But whatever it is, I'm going to do it as me. I need to do something that lets me be my whole self. I think my time with you actually taught me that, Cade, and I'll always be grateful. But I haven't been able to be my whole self with you. We tried to just give one part of ourselves to each other. I don't know about you, but for me, it didn't work."

Dani had said she was coming back, but this felt an awful lot like good-bye. His heart was slowly disintegrating, and he didn't know how to make it stop.

She stood up and turned toward the courtyard entrance. "You know what you said earlier, about how what you wanted didn't matter? That's something I used to think, too. That as long as I was meeting my responsibilities, everything was working out just fine. But then I met you. And I learned that even if someone's going through all the right motions, what they really want matters a whole damn lot." She wiped a tear from her cheek. "I hope you find what you want, Cade."

She left Cade alone, with even more questions than he'd had that morning.

CHAPTER TEN

CADE ARRIVED HOME and slumped into his chair by the fire pit before he even went inside. It had been all he could do to drag himself through his shifts at work over the past few days. The usual things that brought pleasure to his life didn't seem to affect him anymore. Walking along the beach, swimming or watching the sun rise and set no longer gave him joy. Instead, he could barely muster the energy for any of it.

He'd thought about taking some time off work, but ultimately decided against it. If he couldn't be happy, he could at least be useful to his patients.

The only time he'd felt any emotion over the past week was when he'd gotten an e-mail with a "lorovia.gov" address. For half a second, adrenaline had surged through him at the thought that it might be from Dani. But when he opened the e-mail, it was simply a very formal letter from a Lorovian official who'd been designated to be his liaison through "ongoing developments." His child, apparently, was an ongoing development. He supposed he shouldn't be surprised at the formal, careful phrasing. His child wasn't just a child, but also a matter of state for Lorovia. Dani had always implied that that was what royal life was like, but it was strange to experience it firsthand.

It was still difficult for him to even think of having a child without becoming flooded with fear. Dani's words kept coming back to him: Did he think it was best for him to be in his child's life, if he didn't truly want a child? He knew she had a point. As much as he longed to be in his child's life, would his fear of loss prevent him from getting close to a child of his own? Just as it had prevented him from getting close to anyone else in his life?

He missed Dani more than he could have ever imagined. With her gone, it felt as though the sun had left the Caribbean. He hadn't realized how much vitality she brought into his life. For years, he'd done so much alone. He'd eaten lunch alone, spent his days off alone and sat by the fire pit, gazing out at the ocean alone. He missed Dani in the other Adirondack chair next to him. He missed being able to touch her, hold her and feel the heat between the two of them. But most of all, he missed the way they'd been able to work together so smoothly, anticipating each other's needs, and the way she'd always been willing to talk over difficult cases with him. He missed showing her new parts of the island and talking to her after a long day. No matter how warm the weather was, everything felt cold with her gone.

He knew that the gossip surrounding him and Dani was still rampant at work. No one ever spoke about it to him directly, but every time he entered a room, everyone quickly ended their discussions. He wished he could explain, but it wasn't just his secret to talk about. It was Dani's, too, and he hadn't heard from Dani since she left.

The tabloids were getting even worse with their rumors. He'd noticed more photographers on the island lately, eager to get a shot of him. The security at work took care of most of them, but it was irritating to be hounded by press when he was merely trying to go about his business on St. Camille. He'd had several e-mails from tabloids offering him money for exclusive rights to the story of his affair with Dani, which he deleted in disgust.

Dani, for her part, seemed to have completely disappeared from the public eye. He wondered if she was being hounded even worse than he was. He wondered, too, if this kind of attention was something she had to live with anytime she traveled outside of Lorovia. He knew she'd attended medical school under her assumed name, and he was starting to understand, in a way he never had before, why she'd wanted to keep her royal status a secret.

He thought about her facing the scrutiny of the press alone, without him by her side. He wished he could talk to her. But if she wanted to talk, she knew how to reach him. And since she hadn't reached out, he could only assume she preferred to keep him at a distance for now.

He was preparing himself for another lonely evening spent by the fire when his phone buzzed in his pocket. He felt the usual jolt of hope that it might be Dani—but then he saw that it was his mother.

He'd been avoiding the few calls that had come his way lately because he didn't want to respond to any questions, but he knew he couldn't avoid his mother forever.

"Hi, Mom."

"Why, hello there, dear. It's nice of you to answer my call. I hadn't heard from you in so long that I was beginning to worry."

He sighed. "I should have called you sooner."

"You certainly should have. You haven't responded to any of my e-mails, and I've been in a kerfuffle trying to figure out what to do about the wedding."

Wedding? His mother was jumping to some pretty quick conclusions. "Mom, I don't know what you've seen in the papers, but I have no plans to get married."

His mother laughed. "I certainly have seen the papers, and let me tell you, young man, my friends have a lot of questions! And so do I. But that's not what I called to talk about. I called to tell you that I'm getting married."

"What?" He was stunned. After all the conflict he'd witnessed between his parents growing up, the one thing he'd never, ever imagined was his mother getting married again.

"Yes. Irv and I have finally decided that after five years of living together, we want to make it official. We're going to tie the knot. I know this may sound a little unconventional, but I wanted to ask… Would you walk me down the aisle?"

He shook his head, trying to clear his thoughts.

"Mom, are you sure about this? After everything that happened with Dad? After…" He found that he couldn't quite get the word "Henry" out. "After all our family went through?"

"Those were difficult times for all of us, dear. But they were also a very long time ago."

There was a very long pause as Cade tried to

think. He'd always thought that his mother felt the same way he did about relationships: that it was less painful not to get too close. He could understand why she would feel that way, after all she'd been through.

Had he misunderstood her? Had he been wrong?

"Cade? My friends have been asking me if that's you, in those pictures with the Lorovian princess. I don't mean to pry, dear. I know how you like to keep personal things private. But if I'm about to have a grandchild, I'd really prefer to hear about it from you, rather than the headlines."

He sighed. "I don't know how to explain, Mom. It's very complicated. But…yes. There's going to be a child."

"Well, then how complicated can it really be? It sounds very exciting to me."

"How can you say that?" he blurted. His words came in a rush. "How can you call it exciting when you know how it feels to lose a child of your own? Our entire family fell apart once Henry was gone. How could I possibly look forward to this when there's so much to lose?"

"I understand what you're saying," she replied. "You were just a little boy when we lost Henry. It was too much for you to go through and probably too hard to understand what all the adults around you were feeling. But you know what? If I could go through it all over again, I wouldn't change a thing."

"How can you say that? Even knowing what you know now?"

"Because, dear. What I know now is that you don't pass up a chance for love in the present, just because of what happened in the past."

"I don't understand you, Mom. You more than anyone should be worried about what happens if it all goes wrong again."

"Oh, my dear boy. You've got it all wrong. You know, your father and I were having problems in our marriage long before Henry passed, and losing him was not the reason our marriage didn't last. I know those were painful times for all of us. But I'm not afraid of repeating those times. What I'm afraid of is missing out on a wonderful relationship, just because of one bad one that's been over for a long time. I've got a chance to have real love in my life, and dearest, I could lose that chance if I only think about what could go wrong."

He'd never thought about relationships that way. He'd thought his experiences with Susan, and everything he'd seen between his parents, had been a lesson in how relationships inevitably ended.

But Dani had shown him something new. In

spite of all his efforts not to get attached to her, she'd brought a freshness, an excitement, into his life. Being with her had felt different from anyone he'd ever been with. Maybe a relationship with her would have been different, too.

"So you really wouldn't change anything?" he said. "Even knowing what you know now?"

"I'd choose it all again in a heartbeat. Maybe some of my choices were mistakes, but those choices led me to you and Henry. Loss hurts, dear, but it hurts because the good stuff is so good. And I wouldn't give the good stuff up for anything."

He hadn't known his mother felt this way. He'd always thought that, like him, she wanted to protect herself from the pain of loss.

"I'm not as afraid of loss as I am of missing out on my chance at love," she continued. "And I'm afraid of that for you, too."

He thought for a long moment.

From a purely logical perspective, nothing his mother was saying made sense. It certainly wasn't what he'd expected to hear from her.

But from an emotional perspective, he understood every word.

His mother was voicing thoughts that had been nagging at his mind since Dani left. He'd tried to ignore them because they didn't make sense. If he knew exactly how painful heartbreak was, then wasn't he making the logical choice by doing everything he could to avoid it?

He hadn't expected his "logical" choice to hurt this much. And deep down, he understood why. He hadn't wanted to let himself understand because he was afraid. Of pain, of loss, of making the same mistakes all over again.

He'd known he was afraid, but he hadn't wanted to admit it to himself. But what was the alternative? Losing everything because he was afraid to take a chance? Losing his child, and Dani and a real chance at love?

More than a chance. He loved her. Of that he was certain. And if his mother, who had been through so much, could take the risk of opening her heart to love, then so could he.

"Mom," he said, "I think I've made a really big mistake."

"Well, mistakes are part of life. Is there anything you can do to fix it?"

"I don't know. What if I try, and it turns out it's too late?"

"Then at least you'll know you've tried."

Dani could tell the palace photographer wasn't happy. She'd been sitting in the palace photo salon for hours, and the photographer had the defeated air of trying to make the best of a bad situation.

"If you could just try to smile," the photographer said, for what felt like the hundredth time.

Dani forced her lips into an upward curve, but the photographer shook her head in defeat. "Something's not right. Maybe it's the light in here."

"Maybe it's time for a break," her grandmother said. "Give us the room." The photographer bowed and left.

Dani knew the problem wasn't the light. The problem was *her*. She'd been home for a week, and nothing had felt right since she'd arrived. She missed her work and the serene peace of the Caribbean. Worst of all, she'd thought about Cade every day, and her heart ached for him.

She was wearing a full gown and was bedecked with crown jewels. She twisted one of the emerald rings on her finger. No matter how fine her princess regalia was, she couldn't hide the fact that she was heartbroken. She could smile with her mouth, but not her eyes.

She and her grandmother were spending the day together, doing a photo shoot for pictures that would accompany a palace press release announcing Dani's pregnancy. As she was at about twelve weeks, the palace had to make some sort of announcement about her situation. The royal publicist had determined that the best way to deal with Dani's pregnancy would be to portray

Dani as an independent, free-spirited woman who had her life completely under control and was deciding to raise a child on her own. Apparently, the best way to depict that her life was under control was for Dani to be photographed in a gown and tiara, indicating her family's support, acceptance and total control of the narrative. "If she looks beautiful enough, everyone will be so caught up discussing the dress she's wearing that they won't be interested in spreading gossip around her decisions," the publicist had explained, and members of her family had all agreed.

But Dani was having a difficult time mustering the enthusiasm needed to play her part. Her heart was still in the Caribbean, with her work, her friends...and with Cade.

The pins holding her tiara in place made her head ache, and she rubbed her forehead to ease the tension.

"Let me help you with that," said her grandmother, sitting down beside her. She pulled out the pins and removed the tiara. Dani sighed in relief as the tightness eased from her scalp. "Danielle-Genevieve. I've known you since you were born. And I can tell when you're not happy."

"I'm sorry, Grandmother. I'm trying my best."

Her grandmother sighed and reached out to

tuck a loosened strand of hair behind Dani's ear. "I know, dear. You've always tried to do what was right by the family. But your decisions recently have made me see things in a new light. This passion for medicine…this child that's on the way…"

"I know it's not what you expected."

To Dani's utter surprise, her grandmother laughed. And as her laughter continued, Dani grew more baffled. Surely her grandmother, the head of a family that had emphasized tradition and protocol her entire life, couldn't be laughing at such a moment.

Seeing Dani's confusion, her grandmother stopped laughing and grew more serious. "I only laugh, my dear, because you are so right. You've never been what any of us expected, despite your attempts to uphold your duty— and tradition. But having a baby changes everything, doesn't it? It can certainly change the way one sees duty and responsibility." She placed a warm hand on Dani's shoulder. "And even though you've always taken your responsibility toward this family seriously, sometimes I think the pressure we've placed on you has made you forget that you have a responsibility to take care of yourself, too."

"What do you mean?"

"I mean that I've been very impressed by you,

Danielle-Genevieve. By your passion for medicine and your determination to care for your child, no matter what anyone else thinks. Our family may be based on tradition, but if traditions are to survive, they have to be adaptable."

Dani's eyes widened in surprise.

"That diamond necklace you're wearing, for example. It belonged to my great-grandmother. But I have a feeling a stethoscope would make more sense around your neck, my dear."

"Do you mean it?"

"Yes. Let's assume that your decision to be a doctor is a permanent one. And there's no need to have you practice in secret anymore. We all thought the tabloids would get carried away with the story of one of our family holding a profession—in the medical field, no less—but clearly that's been eclipsed by a much more sensational story. It's a silver lining, I suppose. Her grandmother chuckled. "Do you think you'll finish that cardiology fellowship?"

Dani couldn't meet her grandmother's eyes. "I want to, but I don't know if I can ever go back there."

"This is about more than cardiology, isn't it? This is a true matter of the heart."

"I'm afraid so."

As much as her grandmother's understanding meant to her, it didn't ease her heartbreak. She'd missed Cade every day since she got back to Lorovia. She missed his sun-bleached hair, his cinnamon scent and the way he winked when he smiled.

She knew why he was afraid to be in his child's life. He was afraid of loss. But fear of loss was only one side of a coin.

And even if he did try to fight through his fears and be there for their child, it didn't mean he felt anything for *her*.

Tears began to prick her eyes, as they often did when she thought of Cade. Dammit. Now she was going to have to have all her makeup redone if she wasn't careful.

"I'll give you a few moments to collect your thoughts before the photographer comes back in," her grandmother said, leaving Dani to herself.

Dani was grateful to be alone.

As she dabbed at her eyes with the corner of a handkerchief, she heard the door swing open again. Assuming that the photographer had come back, she said, "I'm going to need just a few more minutes to get my game face on."

"That's a shame. I always thought your regular face was perfect."

"Cade!" She was stunned. "How did you get here?"

"I finally responded to the palace liaison who

e-mailed me. After I filled out a metric ton of paperwork, flew here and had my picture taken a half dozen times, they let me up here to see you."

A security guard had accompanied him. "Is it all right for him to be here, Princess?"

"Yes, of course. Give us some privacy, please."

The guard nodded and left.

"I can't believe you're here."

"I hope it was all right for me to come."

"Well…why did you come?"

"Isn't it obvious?"

She raised her eyebrows. "Not to me."

"You're right. I have a lot to explain." His mouth worked, and she could see he was trying to find the right words. Finally, he said, "I can't think of the right way to say this, so I'll just spit it out. I'm an idiot, Dani. An absolute fool. I've done the stupidest thing I could possibly do, and I don't know if it's too late to fix my mistake, but I had to come here to try."

"What mistake?"

"There are so many, actually. It's hard to pick just one. But here's the biggest one of all. I pretended to you, and to myself, that I wasn't in love with you."

Dani was glad she was sitting down, because

all of a sudden, she was trembling all over. She didn't think she'd be able to stand if she tried.

He loved her?

He walked over to her and knelt next to her chair, so that they were at eye level with one another.

"I know we said no emotions. I know we promised each other we wouldn't get attached. But it happened. I fell in love with you. It was impossible for me to know you and not love you. And I'll understand if you don't feel the same way. But I couldn't stand the thought of never telling you. It was a risk I was willing to take, even if I got crushed. Because the fear of risking my heart is worse than the fear of missing out on love."

"Then you mean—"

"I mean that no matter what you feel for me, I'm going to be a father to this baby. I want this child more than anything I've ever wanted in my life, but I was afraid to admit that because I was afraid of loss. But even more than that, I'm more afraid of not giving this child my whole heart. And I'll give it to you, too, if you'll have it. If you want it."

Tears almost made it impossible for her to speak, but she managed to choke out, "More than I've ever wanted anything."

He kissed her, then, and the feeling of his

lips against hers felt like a promise. His arms wrapped around her, and for the first time since she'd returned to Lorovia, she felt as though she was home, really home. The familiar scent of cinnamon that wafted from his neck reminded her of all that could be waiting for her, back in a certain cottage by the sea. Where she'd learned that what she wanted did matter, and was incredibly important, after all.

Finally, they broke apart. Her makeup really was ruined now, and she didn't care the tiniest bit.

"I hope I wasn't too late," said Cade.

"No, Cade. I love you, too…and you were just in time for me to tell you. But are you sure you want all this?" She motioned to the ornate room around her. "You've already gotten a taste of what it's like to have the press involved in your life and some experience with royal protocol. Is it going to be too much?"

He held her face in his hands and looked into her eyes. "Princess Danielle-Genevieve Matthieu DuMaria. I've crossed an ocean for you. I've laid my soul bare for you. I would do so much more. Do you really think filling out a little paperwork could keep me away from the woman I love?"

Love. Her heart thrilled at the word. "But

it's not just a little paperwork. It's quite a few contracts."

He ticked off the items he'd spent the morning completing with the palace liaison. "An NDA, a form that bore a striking resemblance to a *job application*, fingerprints, a background check and an extremely detailed contract in which the palace acknowledges that I will continue my career as a physician—and in which I agree to attend no less than three holiday functions and two state dinners each year—"

"You filled out the consort paperwork!" Her face flamed with embarrassment. "Cade, I'm so sorry. I know all of it's *completely* ridiculous, and I wish royal protocol didn't require it."

He gave her that smile again. The one she knew was real, because it made his eye close in a wink.

He put his arms around her waist and held her close. "All of it is completely inconsequential as long as I have the one thing I really want."

"What's that?" she asked, leaning in to kiss him again.

"Your heart."

"I'm afraid that's impossible," she said, smiling. "I can't give you what's already yours."

EPILOGUE

One Year Later

CADE HAD WORRIED that the warm breeze off the St. Camille coast would threaten the wedding decorations, but everything seemed to be holding up well so far.

As the mother of the prince consort, his mother had been offered palace funds so that she could have a lavish wedding. But she'd eschewed that option for something more personal. Dani and Cade had both been thrilled when his mother chose to have her wedding on St. Camille. It meant that everyone important to them could attend. An eclectic mix of people had come to celebrate the day. In addition to their colleagues from the hospital, Dani's parents and a few other members of the Lorovian royal family were in attendance.

After Dani's grandmother had made it clear that she fully supported Dani's career, the rest of the family accepted Dani's decision. If some of her uncles let slip a few mutterings about "breaking tradition," and "unconventional choices," her grandmother silenced them with a glare and a reminder that traditions without flexibility had outlived their usefulness. Dani and Cade returned to work at the Coral Bay Medical Center, with occasional trips to Lorovia to attend required state functions.

Cade found that life in the public eye wasn't as onerous as he'd anticipated. It helped, of course, that the initial flurry of press coverage and speculation about Dani's pregnancy and mystery consort died down after they married. They'd opted for a quiet ceremony at the palace before returning to St. Camille. The island felt more like home to them than anywhere else, and they both agreed it was the perfect place to raise their child.

At barely three months old, Princess Mathilde-Grace Jeanne Adrienne DuMaria—called Tilly, for short—was the guest of honor at Cade's mother's wedding. And why shouldn't she be? She was perfect.

Cade and Dani sat in the front row, awaiting his mother's walk down the aisle. Tilly fussed a little in Dani's arms. He leaned over and held a finger out to her. Her little fingers curled around his, just as they'd done every day since the day she was born.

All tests indicated that Tilly was in perfect health. Cade, of course, continued to experience the fears of every parent. He was a doctor, after all. He knew that life offered no certainties. But at least he didn't have to worry about his daughter's heart. By all indications, Tilly's was fine.

Her lungs were also in excellent condition. He was relieved that Tilly had finally stopped crying just before the priest leaned over to him and said, "It's time."

He kissed Dani on the cheek and went to the back of the aisle, where his mother was waiting. She'd asked him to walk her down the aisle.

His mother had forgone a traditional white dress for colorful Caribbean garb. She wore a dress with a loose skirt, and a crown of flowers in her hair. She took Cade's arm with a smile.

"Are you ready?" he asked her.

"As I'll ever be."

He walked her down the aisle, his eyes on Dani. She'd looked so beautiful on their own wedding day. But not nearly as beautiful as she did now, with Tilly in her arms.

As they reached the end of the aisle, Tilly grew increasingly fussy. "Go on, dear, if you need to," his mother muttered. "It's all right."

He squeezed her hand in appreciation and sat

next to Dani, trying to calm Tilly down. Dani handed the baby to him and she calmed immediately, as she nearly always did.

"Such a daddy's girl," Dani whispered, smiling.

Unfortunately, Tilly's calm was short-lived. Her cries were so loud that Dani and Cade decided to slip away from the ceremony and walk down the beach.

"Oh, dear," said Dani, embarrassed. "I hope your mother won't be too upset."

"Mom will understand," said Cade. Thinking of the way his mother had only had eyes for her groom, he added, "She might not have even noticed."

"Oh, I think everyone noticed," Dani replied, bouncing Tilly up and down. "This girl has got a set of lungs on her. Hasn't anyone ever told her that princesses are supposed to be quiet and demure?"

"I have a feeling she doesn't much care for what princesses are supposed to do. She takes after her mother in that way."

He took Tilly, finally quietened, and held her close, turning her toward the ocean. "You see that, sweetheart? That's the world. And I'm going to show it all to you. There's so much you won't want to miss out on."

"She's got time," Dani said. "But what about

the two of us? How are we going to make the most of the time we have?"

He wrapped his free arm around her waist and pulled her close. "I have a few ideas." They shared a slow, deep kiss, and Cade felt the rest of the world begin to melt away, as it always did whenever she was close to him.

"You know one great thing about being a princess?" she murmured. "With so many of my family members on the island right now, there's a lot of Lorovian security detail here. Which means we can ask one of them to baby-sit for us."

"Are we going to need a babysitter tonight?"

She traced the lapel of his tuxedo with one finger. "I can almost guarantee that we are." The sun began to make its way down the horizon, turning the sand on the beach into a deep, burnished gold.

They sat down together on the sand, Cade tucking Tilly into the crook of his arm. Dani smiled.

"A minute ago you were saying you wanted Tilly to see the world. But you're holding her awfully tight right now."

"Well, she needs to understand the most important thing first."

"And what's that?"

"How to recognize love when she sees it. And

how to grab on as tight as she can when it's right in front of her."

"Even if she's afraid of losing everything?"

"Especially then. Because that's when you know what's most important." His brow furrowed. "I hope she grows up to understand."

Dani dropped her head against his shoulder, and he put his arm around her.

She tilted her face up toward his. "Every child has their own journey," she said. "She'll make her own mistakes, eventually. But until then, it's up to us to show her what love looks like."

"Well, at least we can handle that," he said. "Because I won't be passing up a single opportunity to show that I love you. Every day, every hour, every moment."

He leaned forward and met her lips with a kiss. Behind them, not far down the beach, they could hear the last few words of the ceremony concluding and the applause from the attendees.

Loss might come, Cade knew. There was no avoiding it. But he was going to teach his daughter how to make the most of her life. When she found love, she wouldn't run from it. She'd run toward it with both arms outstretched.

Just like him.

* * * * *